To Aunt Roberta—
Thank you for everything!

UNREGISTERED

M. LYNCH

M. Lynch

D1382862

CITY O
PRESS

UNREGISTERED
Unregistered, Book 1

CITY OWL PRESS
www.cityowlpress.com

Cover Design by Olivia at MiblArt. All stock photos licensed appropriately.

Edited by Amanda Roberts.

For information on subsidiary rights, please contact the publisher at info@cityowlpress.com.

Print Edition ISBN: 978-1-944728-55-7

Digital Edition ISBN: 978-1-944728-56-4

Printed in the United States of America

To Ryan,
full of faith

CHAPTER ONE

BRISTOL RAY DID NOT EXIST.

At least, not according to official records. The back of his left wrist, where his assigned watch would have lived if his birth had been important, was bare. There was a lump under the skin of his right hand where a tracking chip had been inserted, but he was pretty sure that was there just to scare people like him. He wasn't being tracked. His left hand was ringless, and the skin around his fourth finger was consistent in color and texture to the others. His teeth were hopelessly crooked, his brow prematurely creased, and though the lessons from his mere five years of formal school had faded, his mind was bright with life.

He stood in a shadow, clutching his homemade paper stencil to his chest, and surveyed his work on the brick wall before him. He'd painted a figure that could have been a nun. A slouching, ancient woman dressed in long robes, slicing her chipped hand open with a cross she held in the other. Getting the blood to drip from that hand hadn't been easy. For weeks he had sketched as he watched water drip from faucets to catch a glimpse of that line, that light, and once he'd seen it, his incinerator ate the drafts and roared with rejection. If his incinerator were here and had the ability to destroy whole walls, even this nun may have met her doom. Eventually, though, the nun and her blood had to go out into the world, fully ready or not. He stepped back from it, still safely out of range of the disabled street camera. One could never be too careful.

One last glance over his shoulder was all he allowed himself. She could be there for another week, or she could be gone in a few hours when the morning sun revealed her to the commuters and schoolchildren and stunned police. He packed his stencils and paints in his backpack, kissed the air in her direction, and started home.

Bristol zigged and zagged along the dark streets in the way he always did to avoid the detection of the street cameras. He wore a glove on his left hand with an ice pack slipped inside to cool his chip, just in case. Now that it was no longer activated by his body heat, he was free from all surveillance. The only thing an unregistered person had to lose by breaking curfew was his or her life, which could happily be taken from anybody stupid enough to be caught.

A notice fluttering on a telephone pole read:

WARNING
Any persons not assigned to the artist vocation are prohibited from painting, sculpting, drawing, or working with any other mediums in the attempt to imitate Art. Violators will be prosecuted.

He hesitated a beat, snatched the notice, and added it to his bag.

His sister Denver was waiting for him at the window when he reached the house. With one of the shoddily soldered bars missing, he easily squeezed through into the bedroom they still shared. He returned her smile and handed her the notice.

"A violator you are," she said.

"And intend to stay."

"We'll have to get rid of that," she said, but he'd already taken the scissors to cut it into ribbons. She sat on her bed and yawned. "How did the blood go?"

"Not bad. It was better on the last outline, but it's done now, and I can't think about it anymore."

Denver nodded at the shreds of paper. "Better incinerate those before Mom gets up."

"She'll kill me if I don't. You're lucky."

"What, that I'm getting married?"

Bristol nodded. "And moving out."

Denver laid down and pulled the blanket to her chin. "It's not like I have a choice. And Mom's fine to live with, you know, as long as you don't have any sneaky habits."

"I promised to keep Mom out of it."

"Good. She's made a lot of sacrifices for you."

"I know." Bristol kicked softly at his backpack on the floor. He wasn't sure if Denver was trying to make him feel guilty or not, but if that was her purpose, it did the trick. "Did you get your letter today?"

"Don't change the subject."

"I really want to know."

Denver sighed and shifted. "Not yet, but that's okay. I'm sure they're going to pair me with a Four."

"A Three with a Four? You're studying to be an architect. You're saying you could end up with, what, a nurse or data-bot technician or something?"

"I'm sure Metrics will match us in other ways, personality and all that. I know they don't like to mismatch Tiers, but they'll do it in situations like mine."

"What situation?" Bristol asked, but realized the answer as the words came out. "Oh."

"Don't say oh like that."

"Sorry." He unzipped the backpack with a little more force then necessary, took out his stencil, and ripped small pieces from it. The pile containing the bits of the notice grew larger. "It's just that sometimes I forget that my life is always wrecking someone else's."

"My life is not wrecked. I can still be an architect—I'll just have to live in Four housing and stuff. My kid can still be a Three if they do well enough on their four-year-old exams."

"Yeah." Bristol mindlessly ripped away at the stencil. "It's weird your kid won't have a brother or sister."

"I know. I was thinking about that tonight." She propped herself up on her bony elbows. "Do you realize that at the end of our lives, we'll have known each other the longest out of anyone?"

Bristol sat silent for a moment. "What about Mom? You technically knew her a year before you met me."

"But Mom will die when she's seventy-five. Then I'll have spent fifty years knowing her. But then when *I* die, I'll have known you for seventy-four years! You don't know anyone that long unless it's a sibling."

"Lucky us." Bristol gathered the damning notice and piles of confetti that had been his stencils, walked out of their room, and tossed them into the incinerator. He stopped a moment to watch the flames snatch and lick their prey, reducing weeks of work to shapeless ashes that could have been anything else—a recipe card, an ad, a pamphlet on new and exciting ways to save energy. They all became the same once the fire was done with them. When he came back into the room, Denver was already dressed.

"Almost time to get up anyway," she said. "Bristol, does that scare you?"

"What?"

"Mom dying?"

"No." *Yes.* "Everybody has to do it."

"You don't have to worry. I'll take care of you."

Most people, both registered and unregistered, avoided this topic. At the same time, these kinds of thoughts were intriguing—direct thoughts about privilege shared across the divide. Even from Denver, it felt simultaneously coarse and comforting, though they'd never talked in length about their differences in Tier. He didn't like to think about it, and he certainly didn't want to talk about it. Why would she bring it up now?

She's getting married soon.

"You can live with me," she said. "I'll—"

"And what about this new husband of yours? What is he going to think of marrying someone who has a brother? I mean, what are the chances he's even *met* an unregistered? Not good. What's he going to think of you just taking care of me?" A hotness laced his mouth. "I'll tell you what will probably happen when Mom dies. You and me, we'll look at each other and remember seeing the other one in a smaller size, but we won't really know each other as we are. And you'll care more about your new family than me."

They caught each other's eyes. Denver walked over to the mirror and began brushing and pinning her hair. For several minutes, neither spoke.

Bristol rubbed his sore eyes. "It won't be your fault. It's no one's fault. That's just how the world works, Den."

The sun had begun to soak the curtains, so Bristol stood and opened them to let more of it in. With a click, he turned their blue-tinted overhead bulb off and let his eyes adjust to the color of natural light.

"Thank you," Denver said, her fingers still braiding.

"Do you think Fours have blue lightbulbs too?"

"Everyone does. These units were built right after the uprising, so they're designed to only allow the color blue for lighting."

"Why?"

"It was right after the uprising," she repeated. When Bristol made no indication of understanding, she glanced at the holowatch on her wrist. It was silent, so she stood, pushed in her desk chair, and continued quietly. "People were unhappy. Blue lights make it harder to see your veins."

Bristol nodded. Metrics underestimated how much some people needed an escape and would just invent new ways of getting drugs into their bloodstreams.

Denver sat next to him on his bed. "Listen, while we're on Metrics—"

"I know. I have to stop."

"You *have* to. You've been lucky, but it can't last forever. I don't know what Mom would do if—"

"I know, Den."

"You wouldn't have to stop drawing. I'll still bring you paper when I'm married. You can still make things here."

"You know how careful I am." He closed his eyes. For as unlikely as her offer to let him live with her had been, he could see it had been honest. *Be nicer.* "But I see your point. I'll stop someday."

Denver stood and lingered by the doorframe. "It's got to be soon. I'll see you after work."

She walked away, and an idea for a painting flashed just behind the space between Bristol's eyebrows. Though his body begged for sleep, his hands, suddenly animated by some unconscious energy, fumbled under the bed for a sketchpad and pencil. He crouched over the paper, hoarding the white space and the possibilities it offered, clutched tight the idea in his mind, and began drawing.

CHAPTER TWO

"THIS IS A MIRACLE." SAMARA'S FATHER STARED AT THE LETTER he'd taken from his daughter's hands. "It's...unbelievable."

They'd expected Samara's career assignment just after her twentieth birthday nearly a month ago. Samara and her parents worried, of course, but expected her to receive the same career as her parents—compost collectors—and comforted each other with phrases like *glitch in the system* and *lost in the mail*. Now, it seemed, the Office of Employment had been busy on her behalf.

Samara took the letter back and read it again. No doubt about it. The words were there in black and white:

Dear Ms. Shepherd,
Congratulations! You have been assigned to the career of:

EDUCATION MANAGER
For further details, please report to the Office of Employment on Monday, June 20. The status of your current Tier will be discussed at this time.

Signed,
THE OFFICE OF EMPLOYMENT

"My daughter, the teacher!" Mrs. Shepherd beamed at Samara.

"Mom, no one says *teacher* anymore. They don't really teach, they just...you know...hand out tests and stuff."

"It's still a very important assignment," Mr. Shepherd said and put his arm around his wife. She broke away and scurried to the kitchen, mumbling something about dinner.

Mr. Shepherd looked after her. "Your mother is very proud of you."

"Do you know anyone who's moved Tiers?"

He pursed his lips. "No, I don't."

"Could this be fake?"

Samara held the letter to the light and went through a checklist: the familiar blue ink of Metrics, yellowish paper, the seal at the top, the signature at the bottom. She lowered the letter to find her father staring at her.

"You'll find that out on Monday, I guess."

"I guess."

"Well, put it away for a sec." He winked. "Got something to show you."

She didn't have to ask what it was. With sly smiles and quick glances down at their watches, they walked to the hall window as if summoned. Mr. Shepherd put out a delicate hand to draw open one of the sun-rotted curtains, and Samara let out a long, low sound.

"Beautiful, isn't it?" her father whispered.

"What's that she's got in her hand?"

"It's called a cross. Symbol of an old religion."

Samara blinked at him. "Religion?"

Her father scoffed and put a hand on his neck. "It's too hard to explain. I'm not even sure I understand it. I think it was just something to control the masses back in the day before Metrics."

"So what do you think it's saying?"

"Cutting out her chip..."

"It's only the unregistered who have chips, right?"

He shook his head. "No, they stopped chipping them...it's been ten years ago now. It wasn't very efficient. Those poor guys don't have much left that Metrics can take from them anyway. They step one toe out of line and then—" He snapped his fingers. "Lights out for them. I see some older ones with the bump under their hand, but I'm not sure if they're still monitored or not. And they still chip some people, like long-term hospital patients and prisoners and weirdos who just won't wear their watches. And I think there *are* still some of these religious people around. They probably get chipped too." He turned to his daughter with a full-faced grin. "Hey! I know what it means!"

"What?"

"She just got her employment assignment. She's going to be a surgeon."

Samara jabbed him in the ribs with her elbow and snickered. He laughed a little too loudly.

"What's going on in there?" her mother shouted from the kitchen.

"Dad just told himself a joke!"

"Oh, Richard!"

"I'll tell you later!" Mr. Shepherd called to his wife. He leaned in and whispered to his daughter, "Thanks a lot. Now I have to think of a joke."

"You'll manage."

"Ooh, I'll *manage*. You're talking more like a Three already. Maybe you'll get paired with one now."

"I haven't even decided whether or not I'm going to apply for marriage."

"Well, you don't have to if you don't want to. It's a free country. But it's nice, especially when you finally start to understand each other."

Samara turned back to the window. "Look at the way it moves."

"What?" He looked out the window again.

"Her blood, it looks like its flowing. And the expression on her face, like she's been caught."

At the mention of that word, both watches flashed blue. They backed away from the window as if it had burst into flames.

"Won't catch *me* in that kitchen, Samara!" Her dad's register had become lower. "Your mother is working hard, and I'll stay out of her way!"

"You will?" Mrs. Shepherd walked out of the kitchen and into the hallway. She rounded the corner, still scrubbing a squash. "That doesn't sound much like—oh." She stopped at the sight of the flashing watches. "Well, it'll all be ready in about half an hour. Don't you two have things to do?"

Samara shrugged. "Homework," she said and disappeared into her room.

It wasn't a lie. She had enough reading tonight to make her eyes quiver, though no one at school would check if she'd actually done it or not. Still, she worked until dinner and went right back to it afterward, making both her parents beam with pride. *That's our girl, Cora. Obviously they're looking more at merit nowadays than birth.*

Having learned the danger of getting one's hopes up too high, she put the letter out of her head, rested her left wrist on her desk, and found her schoolwork on her watch. After checking that she had the most up-do-date version of the text—it had been edited at 8:01 that morning—she adjusted her eyes to the soft white light and focused on the words projected before her on the desk. Despite looming promises of bleak futures, Fives worked as hard as the other tiers on their exams. Samara did not know what would happen if she didn't pass, and never thought to wonder. She feared failing, of course, and that was enough. She read until she had to reread sentences twice, three times, and four times to understand them.

It was well past curfew when they heard the sirens. Before her brain had registered the sound, her nervous system took over, forcing her heart to race and her brow to sweat. Like her peers, she had been raised with a healthy fear of the police. She crouched down, and staying low to the ground, followed the sound. It was loudest in the hall.

Her parents were already there, waiting on either side of the window. Her mother held out her arms to draw her into them while her father held a finger to his lips. He glanced out.

"What's happening, Dad?"

"They got him." His face was long and solemn. "They—"

He was cut off by a violent symphony, the sounds of batons beating skin, laughter from many, screams from one.

"Poor fella."

"Get him in the car!" said a voice from outside, and in a matter of seconds, the air was still again. They looked at their watches. Mr. Shepherd's was the first to talk.

"Incoming message," said a woman in a cool, robotic tone. He touched the face. "The vandal accused of defacing the walls of the number seventeen housing unit in your area has been arrested. Please avert your eyes from the graffiti until it has been cleaned. Thank you."

They'd heard it before. The same words every time, meant to comfort or threaten—the robot woman's tone never hinted toward either. This time, however, there was something new. A hologram of a boy's face appeared in the air before them.

Mr. Shepherd's eyes were downcast. "They must have got him, all right."

Before this boy's face, there was just the message.

Later, without fail, another painting would adorn the same wall.

CHAPTER THREE

"WE'RE SPEAKING WITH DR. BRUCE KATCHUM, DISTINGUISHED professor of history at Cola-Rite University." The brilliantly clad news anchor widened her eyes and cocked her head to the side. "Cola-Rite! It just tastes right."

The logo appeared at Bristol's feet, along with a code, which could be swiped by a watch to have the drink delivered within ten minutes. But Bristol was watching the hologram of the gray-bearded man projected before him.

"Great to be here, Melissa."

"Professor, let's dive in. You claim that as recently as a hundred years ago, this story wouldn't even have been reported as news."

The man smiled. "That's right! Back then, a police force would have made hundreds of arrests in a single city in a single day. Crime was so rampant that graffiti was the least of their concerns."

Melissa snorted. "Times have changed! If you're just joining us now, we're talking about the successful arrest of a local vagrant notorious for defacing the walls of buildings, such as the 52nd street bus terminal"—an image of scientists with paintbrushes stroking the skin of a newborn baby appeared—"Achievement Only Elementary School"—a family portrait with the faces of two of the three children marked out with red Xs—"and, of course, the wall of the number seventeen housing unit"—the nun.

Bristol's heart jumped into his throat and he looked over his shoulder at the window again, half expecting to find a policeman right there to pluck him from home while his mother and sister were still at work. But he was alone, having called the restaurant to tell them he was too sick to cut up their vegetables and wash their dishes and unload their deliveries today. The police weren't releasing details about the suspect, but that didn't stop the national news stations from broadcasting their wild speculation, nor did it stop Bristol from gorging himself on the coverage.

The little hologram of a man shifted in his seat. "People of that time were simply not respectful of their government. Most understood very little, and that majority grew too numerous to tolerate. As I've said, crime was a problem. Thomas Armistead himself was the first leader to offer a reward for sterilization. Many took it, and it left a smaller cohort of citizens who better understood how to live in a manageable society. Shortly after that, the one-child policy was enforced, and now, happily, we have a smaller and smaller amount of people who need our care. You sometimes hear a fuss about how difficult it is for young people to be matched as a result, or that our workforce is dwindling. But consider this: fewer people and more technology is always the better way. This incident has taught us that. With fewer people, you have less crime. Young people who are upset about not getting a match should consider that. Life might get a little lonely when you're not married, especially in the short time at the end of the day when you're not at work, but it's good for the country."

The news anchor's eyes flickered down to her watch, then back to the man. "Professor, should we be afraid that others may follow suit?"

The professor chuckled. "Melissa, Melissa, Melissa... This man— a confessed criminal—will be jailed for the rest of his life. Any copycats will only have to look to him—and to the unfortunate citizens of the past—to weigh whether or not painting on the walls is really worthwhile."

Now it was the news anchor's turn to laugh. "Thank you. Up next, we know that this wall has been the target of graffiti before, but no one has reported it. Who's to blame? We'll talk to residents of the number seventeen housing unit who say, *not them!* And we'll ask—" She raised one sharply shaped eyebrow "—'Why not'?"

She turned her head and instantly morphed her face into a wide grin. "But now, show your hairdresser some love! It's the first annual hairdresser appreciation day, and it's happening next week. To show you care, give a gift from Gooby's Chocolates..."

Bristol turned off the holovision before he had to endure another commercial. Parts of his brain were buzzing and other parts remarkably still. The paints and brushes that had created the nun painting were still lurking under his bed, but he was here, still a free man, while another man had gone to prison.

He walked into his bedroom in a daze and, from its dark hiding place, picked up the sketch he'd created the night before. It was an image of Denver—though it wasn't Denver's face—arm-in-arm with a blue link, the profile of her future husband. He liked it more than he thought he would, yet now it seemed heavier, the weight of a new life on the thin page.

Bristol let the paper sail down onto his bed. He crouched down and held his fingers to his temples. How many times had Denver warned him that it was a matter of time until something happened? He'd always just assumed that someday he'd come to his senses and paint on paper that nobody saw. Like a regular person.

A regular person. First-born—only born—and registered. He knew he shouldn't allow himself to wallow long in these low thoughts, but it was hard to stop once he got going. Why had his mother even given birth to him knowing that as a second child, he'd be condemned to a life of hard labor with no access to the things that made life worth living? No education, no career, no spouse, no family.

Now that his mind was here, it replayed for him a memory of

particular shame—himself in kindergarten, angry at the teacher for a forgotten reason. As a sort of revenge, he'd drawn a picture of her. Even as a child, he knew what he was doing. He'd heard her talk about losing weight to a coworker and exploited it, drawing her face and dress on a cow's body. The page had no words. Bristol felt, in his five-year-old-heart, that the drawing said it all. He handed it to her as she stood in the threshold.

Her face twitched. "Oh my. I hoped you'd be good at *something*, but now I can see art isn't really your thing either." She tore the page in half, turned to another teacher in the hall, and jerked her head toward Bristol. "Unregistered." She looked at him again with her nose upturned. "Well, Bristol, add art to the list of weaknesses... along with math, reading, science..."

Bristol shuddered on his bedroom floor. *Stop. Stand.* The floor underneath his feet still swayed, but he stood firm. One step at a time.

One step at a time. He'd always had a feeling this might happen, that Metrics might put the blame on some poor slob, and now that it had happened, he felt both oddly possessive of his crimes and sympathetic to the guy holding his place in prison right now. After all, this guy wasn't the one who'd spent hours sketching, plotting new ways to say old ideas. This guy hadn't spent sleepless nights thinking of the best walls in the city to paint. He didn't deserve to pay the price for Bristol's lifestyle and he certainly didn't deserve the martyrdom. That was Bristol's alone to claim. Of course, if this was really a bad guy or something, maybe he *did* deserve to be in jail. Sometimes Metrics knew what they were doing, giving false excuses to get the real bad guys off the streets...

He'd have to find out who this was, make sure this man was innocent before Bristol did anything drastic. He'd have to go back to the wall. Maybe the man had mislaid something, dropped something, left some clue as to who he was and why he was there. Without giving himself a chance to reconsider, he left the apartment with his shoes still untied.

In the daylight, he walked in a straight line on the road like a good citizen and gave a wide berth to anyone passing in the opposite direction. As he approached the wall where she was painted, he noticed a large blue drop cloth hiding her from the public. The blue plastic rippled. Anger rose in Bristol at the thought of someone in there with his nun, probably scrubbing away at her with paint thinner. *I hope you choke on it.* The folds in the drop cloth separated, and a girl about his age stepped out.

She exited quickly, but her eyes darted in both directions like those of a guilty cat. She made it only three steps in Bristol's direction before she noticed his gaze and stopped.

"What?"

"Nothing."

The girl's fingers went to her watch, but it was only to twist it around her wrist. "I wasn't doing anything wrong."

"I won't tell."

"Good."

She walked on, but Bristol turned and followed. "What's back there? Behind the cloth?"

She turned her head but didn't look at his face. "It's a painting. Just a painting. Are you from Metrics?"

He held out his bare wrist and smooth hands. "Do I look like I'm from Metrics?"

She smiled and let out a little breath. "Listen, it's just a painting. Of a nun. It's nice, actually. I can't recommend that you go back there to look, but if you did, you might not regret it."

"Why were you back there? Just curious?"

"No, it wasn't that. I'd seen it before. I just wanted to look because it makes me feel..."

Bristol leaned in as he walked. "Feel what?"

"Still. Calm."

A sound came from Bristol's throat. "How does it make you feel calm? She's cutting herself!"

Now she stopped. Her eyes locked on his. "I didn't say what she was doing."

Her words hung suspended between them for a horrible moment.

If this girl had been a member of Bristol's kitchen gang, he would have just puffed his chest and turned his back to send an *I don't have to explain myself to the likes of you* message. But this girl didn't look angry enough to evoke that sort of response. She looked curious, something he hadn't seen from a stranger before, and it stirred some profound fright in him.

"I saw it on the news. I'm sorry I pretended I didn't know. I saw it..." He kicked a pebble and watched it skid down the sidewalk. "On the news. I promise I don't work for Metrics. I just make soup at a place on 23rd."

She looked down at her own feet and then continued walking. "I shouldn't have said anything at all. You should probably forget this conversation happened."

As it was the first time he'd ever heard anyone apart from Denver talk about his art, this was the last thing he wanted to do. And he still needed answers. "Do you know who did it?"

"Someone was arrested."

"I know, but who?"

"I don't know who he is. But he's just a kid. Bet you didn't see that on the news."

Bristol's eyes widened. "I didn't."

"They're calling him a *man*, but he was a kid. About ten years old." She had stopped in front of a filthy painted metal door, its weight barely supported by the rusty hinges.

Bristol's heart thumped. "Ten..."

"What's your name?"

"Bristol. Yours?"

"Samara." She adjusted her bag on her hip and stood back, relaxed. "Go look at the painting in person, before they paint over it. It will make you feel better."

Samara heaved open the door, her right bicep bulging slightly as if to prove she'd been opening this same door since childhood.

CHAPTER FOUR

DURING HIS INITIAL SENTENCING, JUDE REEDER SAW HIS PARENTS at what he suspected may have been the happiest moment in their marriage.

The session lasted exactly twelve minutes, and most of those minutes passed with no changes to how Jude was used to seeing them: distant, distracted, and annoyed to be putting their lives on hold to spend time in the presence of their son. Then, in front of Jude, the judge told them some unexpected information: now that Jude was to be imprisoned for life, they would be allowed to try for another child. Immediately they turned to face each other and, as if they were seeing each other for the first time in a decade, reached for each other with silent tears welling in their eyes. Jude thought it was an odd reaction, those tears, but when he realized they were laughing, he understood. Since he was very small, he'd had the feeling his parents thought it was unjust that they'd tried for a high-ranking child, as they had both been themselves, and gotten him instead.

Even though he was a Two and was supposed to have superior genes, Jude was useless at running, throwing, catching, kicking, and anything else that required coordination. He wasn't much better at the things that didn't require coordination; at school, he regularly scored in the bottom percentiles because he could never finish the daily tests in the allotted time frames. Worst of all, he was terrible at making friends; even among his fellow losers, he was avoided. His parents noticed. For a few years, they took him to doctors, who injected him with medicine that was supposed to make him stronger, faster, smarter, and more likable. Those attempts always ended in disappointment and frightening side effects, like the time Jude found a long black hair growing from his left eyeball. For the past two years, he'd been living as a piece of old furniture in the house: tolerated but wholly unwanted.

So that was that. His mother did at least say goodbye, though it was rushed because the two female guards were already on either side of him, pulling him through the door. He tried to get one last look at his father's face, but he was looking down at his watch.

The guards put Jude in a driverless little white transport with bars on the windows and shut the door. He rode alone to the place he'd spend the next seven years of his life: Fox County Juvenile Detention Center. It was so rare that Jude was alone, truly alone, that he didn't quite know what to do. He realized he could cry if he wanted to, so he did. Then he realized that with his hands tied behind his back, he wouldn't be able to wipe his tears before he saw the guards who would collect him on the other side.

Who cares?

It wasn't a typical thought for Jude, but this wasn't a typical situation. He said it aloud, to no one, and then again, louder and louder until he was roaring it: "*Who cares?*"

It wasn't until he kicked the floorboards of the transport that it pulled over to the shoulder quick enough to knock Jude's head against the window. "Please stay calm," said a robot voice, disguised as a young woman's. "Transport will resume when blood pressure returns to your body's average rate. Please take five calming breaths."

Feeling the bruise forming on the side of his head, he leaned back and rested on the seat. He inhaled. He exhaled.

It only took a few days for him to stop looking forward to meal times. So far, he'd choked down moldy biscuits, soggy mushrooms, and uncooked corn on the cob. Most of the food he'd come into contact with looked like it had seen its first birthday come and go. But Jude had made the decision that he wanted to stay alive. He'd only *been* alive for eleven years, and even though he wasn't sure what the point of it was, he at least wanted the chance to find out. He came up with a strategy for getting food into his stomach without dry-heaving, and after a few days, when the soreness in his right hand where they'd implanted a tracking chip had worn away, he decided to try out his idea. He held a white plastic spork in his right hand, and he focused on the clock hung high on the cheap drywall.

Albin Kopecky placed his tray across from Jude and lifted one leg over the long bench to sit, but Jude's gaze didn't leave the clock. "What's up, Reeder?"

"Shh."

The slight hand hit twelve, and Jude's spork moved like a hummingbird from his plate to his mouth. With his shoulders hunched over the table and his spine in the shape of a C, he ate, hardly chewing, hardly breathing, until the hand returned back to twelve.

Kopecky gave a chuckle and glanced over either shoulder. "It ain't a race, y'know."

A whole minute to spare, so why not? "It's my new system. You get the calories, but not the taste. You eat in intervals, one minute on, one minute off for four minutes."

"You look like a lunatic."

"I don't care. And anyway, you should probably start trying it out, 'cause they'll probably make it mandatory soon." He nodded toward the camera over his left shoulder, but his eyes were on the clock. "Excuse me."

"What do you—"

But Jude was already speed-eating again, pieces of boiled celery flying down his throat. Kopecky swore softly, bowing his head and avoiding the eyes of all who'd turned their heads. Jude stopped when his food was gone, with six seconds to spare. He blotted the corners of his mouth with a napkin.

"What do I mean by that? I mean that I'm doing this for my sensitive taste buds"—an eye-roll from Kopecky—"but I realize it's very efficient. It won't be long now until the administration understands what I'm doing, adjusts for less rest time, and normalizes it."

"Yeah? They gonna make us talk like pussies, too?"

Jude blinked. "One: they give us twenty-five minutes for lunch, and I finish in four. That's twenty-one wasted minutes when I could be making house numbers or license plates or road signs. They'd be stupid if they missed that, and they aren't. Two: if you wanted to critique me and use expletives, why did you come over at all?"

Kopecky exhaled. "I dunno. Guess I'll get going." He grabbed the tray with both hands and hovered it an inch above the table. He looked over Jude's shoulders at the crowded cafeteria. Jude once again heard the low rumble of conversation, like gravel under tires, and he turned around to look at Kopecky's view. There were some small holes between groups of friends and allies, but no place where a person could eat alone.

The tray popped back down. "Well, why should I go? I'm here now."

Jude leaned over his empty plate. "Nobody likes you."

"So what? Nobody likes *you* neither."

"I know."

"You seem used to it, though."

"Yes. You'll get used to it too."

"I been here for nine years, kid," said Kopecky. "I never did yet."

"You've been eating alone for nine years? Not by choice? How?"

"They're scared of me. Why I'm here."

Jude considered this a moment. Everyone needed a friend, his mother had always said, but needing something and having it were different things. He could just as easily turn people into friends as he could turn them into rabbits. He'd never even been through a real Emotion Talk, although they frequently practiced the script in school. It went like this: *Do you need to talk? Tell me more. What can you do to stop this? I'm glad we talked.* The emotional kid could say whatever they liked, but the friend had to stick to the script. You never know when you can make things worse. Not that Jude ever got the chance. Whatever this boy had done, it seemed silly to waste this opportunity to force someone into getting to know him.

"I'm Jude."

"I know. You're the artist."

Jude frowned. "Well, no..."

"No? Your teacher tell you to meet her there at the wall?"

Jude's back straightened. "The principal."

Kopecky clapped once and threw his head back. "Ha! They set you up!"

"It was a mistake. I'll be out of here as soon as they reach Mr. Richards to testify that I did not—"

"Buddy, Mr. Richards went back to his own miserable life after he followed those orders to get you locked up." He took a bite of mashed potatoes the consistency of melted ice cream without grimacing. "Happens all the time. Who'd you piss off?"

"What?"

"Someone had it out for you. Usually it's schools weeding out the kids they know will end up here in a few years anyway. Sometimes parents. So who hated you?"

Jude's mouth hung open. He had done exactly nothing except what Mr. Richards asked him to do. The message that had flashed on his watch was *Meet me at this address at 9 tonight.* Yes, it had seemed odd and it was after curfew, but why would he have questioned it? If he'd learned one lesson in school, it was that you didn't question things adults told you to do.

Kopecky slurped up the last of his potatoes and then set his spork down. "Do you need to talk?"

Jude inspected Kopecky's face for signs of deviousness, but saw nothing he recognized, as usual. Yes, he wanted to talk. He wanted to tell someone that he was sure Kopecky was wrong but that he was also terrified Kopecky was right. He wanted to talk about how his parents were happy to be rid of him, how the last word he'd heard from his mother's lips was a flat *'bye*, and how he couldn't remember the last time his father had spoken to him and not about him. He wanted to tell Kopecky he wasn't really used to people not liking him, either, and that he had no idea why he felt this nonsensical desire to stay alive. He hoped he'd be able to get out of here, since he was innocent, maybe even advocate for himself the next time he had a hearing. Maybe then his parents would be proud of him. Maybe they'd get to have another baby anyway, and then he could have a brother. He wanted to tell Kopecky all of this, but the soreness of his right hand was distracting him, and they seemed to have next to nothing in common anyway. He wouldn't understand. Best to play it safe. "No. But thank you for asking."

CHAPTER FIVE

"I DON'T UNDERSTAND."

Samara sat with her hands folded on her lap under the chilly stainless-steel table. The employment officers exchanged looks, perhaps not having rehearsed an alternative message. They looked like male and female versions of each other, each in a crisp uniform with gold buttons gleaming on dark blue wool. Matching hairstyles, each with a large swoop at the front, though his was cropped short in the back and hers was gathered tight into a second swoop of a bun. The man tapped his pristine fingernails.

"Samara, what we're saying is that we're proud of the employment offer we made to you. You deserve it. Our concern is in your potential for actual employment. Schools do not generally hire teachers that do not meet all the standard requirements."

"Yes, I worried about that too. But I wasn't able to attend a Tier-Two or above high school, because I went to a Tier-Five middle school. And elementary school. And preschool..."

"Of course," the female said with a wave of her hand. "It is a difficult situation. But we stand by our system. It does not make mistakes. You will be working in education, Miss Shepherd. The question is, where?"

Samara leaned forward. "Why am I here?"

"We're offering you a choice. You can either work in a school or in an alternative environment. In the school, you'd be responsible for cleanliness. Bathrooms, hallways, the cafeteria, anyplace where students learn."

A janitor. Unregistered work. Samara saw her imagined future—the one where she had students and a big desk and a bag of papers to take home every night—fly away from her suddenly, like a ball thrown into the distance. One minute it's solid reality, the next, a speck in the sky.

"In the alternative environment, you'll be responsible for student learning."

"What's this alternative environment?"

"A prison for young boys."

"When do I start?"

She spent the bus ride home trying to sit like the employment officers—back straight, shoulders together but relaxed—and reviewed her packet of information on classroom management. Managers, she read, usually spent two years in formal training, but since the Fox County Detention Center had an immediate opening, she'd taken the final test right there at the employment center...with a sheet of answers just to the left of her paper. They must have needed someone badly.

When she was sure she'd memorized where to go and when, she leaned the side of her forehead on the bus window and looked out, but she didn't see anything in particular. Her mind was on her future students. She'd never been in a prison before, though she'd heard plenty of stories of those who ended up there. In recent years, they'd been taking women who'd had one child already but were pregnant again and refused to have an abortion. There had been one such woman at her mother's workplace. Two men in shiny blue uniforms came and put a bag over the woman's head. That afternoon, she got an abortion and a ten-year sentence.

She knew nothing of boys and what they'd have done to deserve imprisonment, save for the one taken away in cuffs for painting the nun. She'd probably meet him.

A ray of electricity ran under her skin, like her body had realized this just before her brain. Of course she would. Why wouldn't she? He was caught in Fox County and sentenced here too. Surely there was only one center in the county where he could have gone. Imagine! All those times looking out the window and seeing the wall with another painting on it, trying to figure out what he was trying to say, running her eyes over the lines, the color, the depth that he somehow managed to create with just bricks and paint—then to be his teacher! *No, Manager, remember.*

She'd even seen him once. It was a bit like seeing Santa Claus, she guessed, back when people celebrated Christmas. She'd woken in the middle of the night, not to an alarm but to a feeling, like her dream had ended and the credits rolled and it was just time to leave the theater. She had looked out her unit's window on a whim and saw something new—a cat with the flag of the Ones in its teeth. It wasn't until she'd had a good look at the cat that she saw the boy looking at the wall and twirling a paintbrush in one hand. He must have been big for his age because she didn't think he was a kid. Then again, lots of kids were bigger than they were in the movies, and that was really the only place one saw children. He was tall and slightly thick with darker skin than usual, and he'd seemed to be in perpetual motion while he worked—swaying, twirling, darting close to and away from the bricks. Though it had been the only time Samara had really seen him, she felt like she knew him.

Every painting that appeared by his hand felt like it was just for her. The wall was there to identify with her, like the time she'd gotten into a fight with her best friend, Georgia, and felt so alone, then looked out her window to see hands reaching toward each other in a swirl of colors. It was there to mock her, recognizing the false parts of her with shrewd precision, like the few weeks she'd spent more time playing games than talking to her family, then saw a painting of a young child staring down at his watch against a collage of all the beautiful elements of nature; dazzling clouds and shockingly green trees. For the past three years, the paintings on the walls had been her source of comfort, and she cheered the artist on as if he were a close friend. As far as she was concerned, he was.

The bus stopped, and Samara stepped into the street in a very different world than the one she'd just been in. There, in the Two neighborhood, the sidewalks were white, with clean-cut green hedges marking the medians between the pedestrian, bike, and vehicle lanes. Sculptures of life-sized bronze bodies stood intermittently along the hedges. Artists—assigned to the profession —had undoubtedly created them. The bronze citizens were all doing something to represent Metrics values—one flexing his biceps for Resilience, one sitting and staring at the ground for Silence, one standing at attention for Obedience. Here, where the Fives lived, the wind stank of smoke and blew crumpled trash along the gray pavement.

Mrs. Harris squatted on a plastic stool in front of her convenience store just in front of the bus stop. She saw Samara and called, "Your dad was lookin' for you! Where you go?"

"I had a meeting." Samara's brow furrowed. "He knew about it."

"Maybe he forgot."

"Thanks, Mrs. Harris."

Samara walked briskly back to the apartment, huffing not with exertion but with annoyance. The day a girl found out how she would spend every day of the rest of her life was a day for a thoughtful stroll, maybe along the side of the street with the sidewalk. Instead, she was rushing home, probably because Mom wasn't back yet and Dad had forgotten the temperature to bake a potato.

She heaved open the door, ran up the steps, touched the doorknob, and stopped. She had to catch her breath a moment to be sure, but after a few seconds, she was certain. Her father was crying on the other side.

She made a fuss of finding the right key and putting it into the door in hopes that her dad would hear the jingle of the metal and pull himself together. But when she finally walked in, he was still struggling to steady his breath. He walked over to her and pulled her into a hug before she had a chance to hang her bag on the hook.

"I'm so glad you're home," he said.

"Where's Mom?"

Her dad squeezed tighter. Then he broke away. "While you were away, some Metrics officials came to the door. They told us that our employment needed to change to compensate for yours. With Mom and me in Five jobs and you working in a Three position, our household income would..." He picked up the first page of a neat little packet sitting on the table and read, "...'exceed the limits of our Tier.' So they had to take one of us to work outside the city."

"They took Mom?"

Her dad sniffled. "I wanted them to take me, but they did it based on citizenship score. I don't know how hers could be lower. We have the same friends. It must be someone at her work that's brought her down."

Samara could hear herself breathe. "Do you know where she is exactly?"

"Near Fallwood, they said. Where the berry farms are. She'll pick blueberries until the harvest is over. Then she'll be moved somewhere else. She's allowed to keep her watch, even though reception isn't great out there. She says she'll let us know when she gets there."

Samara said nothing and looked at a scuff mark on the linoleum.

"It's not forever. Just until you apply for a spouse and get married. She can come back when you're in a house of your own."

"Not until then?"

"Well, we could pay a fee. It's expensive, though. Basically a year's worth of income for the three of us put together."

Samara perked up. "Maybe I'll get a bonus or something! I'll work hard and get a raise."

Her dad hugged her again. "This isn't your fault, you know. Your mother and I don't blame you," he said, but then he stood, walked into the room he had shared with his wife, and left Samara standing by the front door alone.

CHAPTER SIX

DENVER LET THE LETTER FALL TO THE BATHROOM FLOOR.

It had come a day early, just as she'd hoped it would. Though Mom and Bristol weren't home yet, she'd still retreated to the most private room in the house before opening it. She stared at it, the ramifications of the blue printed words only now washing over her.

His name was Stephen Steiner. His skin and hair were very light, which she expected, being darker-skinned herself—Metrics liked to mix skin colors so eventually all people would be exactly the same color. They'd done a remarkably good job at it so far, though Denver and Bristol somehow turned out darker than their parents. He was also in Mid-Tier Four, a full Tier beneath her. She'd expected that too. A dead father and a live brother made her a poor match for a Three. Mr. Steiner was studying to work as a dispatcher for the Department of Transport, which meant they spent every day in the same building. Had she seen him before? All those days rushing through the door for her daily seven a.m. meeting, all those glassy-eyed elevator rides, the trips home where she simply shut off the part of her brain that cared about being shoved and smashed by the current of commuters. Was he there among them?

Maybe. There was a link to his profile on the paper, of course, and scanning it would make his face appear right here in the bathroom with her. Then she would recognize him, or not. No, she'd let it go. It was enough for one evening to understand the irritating reality that she would go live with a stranger. Seeing a strange face would only make reality itch more.

A knock at the bathroom door made her jump. "Yes?"

"It's me, honey," Mom said. "Everything okay?"

Denver opened the door and looked into her mother's face. Mom looked down at the letter. Both watches flashed with light. Of course. Just when she wanted to really talk...

"My letter came! He's a dream! Isn't it wonderful?" said Denver.

"Let's celebrate tonight!"

"Perfect!"

The flash only signaled the start of the recording, so she couldn't be sure how long they'd listen. The average recording was seven minutes, though at work, she'd listened to recordings of others that had lasted several hours.

Bristol rounded the corner, looking like a storm in his all-black uniform. "What are we celebrating?" His gaze landed on the blue lights at their wrists, and then the letter. "Oh. Congratulations, Den."

"Thank you!"

She rolled her wet eyes and looked again at her watch with a small smile. *Can you believe our luck?* Then she leaned down and took the letter from the floor back into her bedroom. Now that Bristol knew, she was sure he'd give her some privacy.

She leaned her forehead on the cool window. *You're doing everything right.* She'd studied hard and had a solid job waiting for her at Metrics. There was absolutely nothing in the letter she didn't expect. Still, now that she had her letter, she wished it hadn't come today, but tomorrow. The anticipation had tricked her into thinking this enormous life change would be nothing but positive, but now the anticipation was over, she longed for one more day to be just Denver, herself unchanged and her life unremarkable.

The doorknob turned, too slowly to be Bristol. Mom poked her head in the room.

"How long has it been, then?" asked Denver.

"Thirty minutes," said Mom. "If they're still recording, let them listen."

She sat down on the bed and held out her arms. Denver curled into them like a child.

"When I was assigned, everything was different," Mom said. "The whole system was just being built. It wasn't sophisticated like it is now, how they take personality and abilities and past choices into account. They couldn't, really, because the war had drained us and there was no money to relocate people to be near a perfect assignment. They matched us locally, and the only thing they looked at was our skin color. Light with dark. Now it's all different. You two will get along. They'll have made sure. You might even come to love each other."

Denver pulled away and leaned against the wall. "Did you love your assignment?"

Mom licked her lips. "I loved your father."

"You must have. To have two kids with him..." Denver looked at her mother, who was now looking down and twirling a bit of the blanket in her fingers. Denver's mind began to simultaneously speed and slow, as if it were running in the sand. "With Dad. With Don Ray."

Mom buried her left wrist in the blanket and said, "It was different, baby. I thought I'd tell you when you were older, but you might as well know. It was different then. Don—Dad—was a homosexual." She took a breath. "And it wasn't like it is today, where they can just choose to live without a spouse. Back then, everyone of a certain age had to be married. The most important thing was creating the New Race."

Denver stared at the bit of blanket in her mother's hand for a full minute. "He wasn't my real dad." She'd meant to ask it as a question, but it came out like she already knew.

"He was a good man. He was kind and clever and..."

Denver curled her knees into her body. "But I don't have his DNA."

"No. No, baby, you don't. But that doesn't mean I didn't love him in another way. We worked well together, and you'll work well with your assignment too."

"You had two children outside of marriage and Dad killed himself. *That's* why neither of us have the right New Race skin tone. You call that working well together?"

"Don had a lot of problems, honey. He was depressed anyway—he would have been even if we weren't married—and Metrics never made things easy for him."

"*You* didn't make things easy for him either."

"Don encouraged my affair, if you'd call it that. He loved spending time with both you and Bristol. He wanted kids. He just didn't want to make them with me."

Mom tried to touch Denver's shoulder, but Denver dodged her. "Do you want to know who your father is?"

"No!"

And with that, she got up, put on her shoes, and walked out the front door. She briefly registered Bristol standing to stop her, but she charged past him.

She walked into the first cold snap of spring. She hadn't brought her jacket, but the thought of going back to get it filled her with disgust. It didn't matter how hard she fought for a better life, she couldn't escape the fate already laid down for her. She didn't know how Metrics even let her slip through—she should be as unregistered as Bristol, fighting toward nothing, sleeping and eating and going to work without any thoughts of rising or falling. What had Mom been thinking? To have a child with another man, get away with it, and then to have *another*... Of course, Mom's citizenship score was low as tree roots, but did she really believe the punishment would stop with her? How crazy was she to believe she could hide such a thing from Metrics? They kept samples of everyone's blood since birth, so they must have known and decided within an hour of Denver's entrance into the world that she wouldn't live long as a Three. They probably only allowed it to save some face and convince themselves that their matching system was working.

She approached Craft Street, where assigned artisans made specialty coffee and bread and jewelry and other things she soon wouldn't be able to entertain the possibility of buying as a Four. Did Mom realize that? That her daughter's entire way of life was about to change drastically because *she* didn't do the right thing and abort when she had the chance? And then there was the other question of who this man had been. Mom had lived in that apartment since she was twenty. Could it be someone local? Denver scanned the area for men with skin like night. People shopped along the street happily— just another day for them, burning the hours until curfew—but all of these people had about the same paper-bag–brown tone to their skin. She couldn't go on like this. She was suffocating.

Denver sat on a bench with spikes between individual seats. Her gaze found a store window. In it, a bright pink mannequin with splayed arms and legs wore a short green dress, ridiculous for this weather. The fabric looked light and three or so shades of green were layered on top of each other. She didn't particularly like it, but she liked the sight of the store window.

"Watch—current dress size," she said.

A woman's voice answered her from her wrist. "Your current dress size is two."

She held her watch to her eyes, pointing the face toward the window. "Show an image of me in this."

A hologram of herself wrapped in green appeared floating before her eyes. Not bad.

"Buy it."

"Bought."

She tapped the face so she wouldn't have to hear the part where the store owner comes on and thanks you and tries to get you to buy more. She walked up to the clerk, who smiled and handed her the bag. A moment of desire satisfied. It wouldn't last, but with any luck, she'd think of something else when the suffocation came back.

CHAPTER SEVEN

BRISTOL WASN'T ALLOWED TO TALK AT THE RESTAURANT, HIS manager was very clear about that. The kitchen was full of unregs, and by this time in their lives, they'd grown accustomed to always being asked to listen, but never talk. When they found communication absolutely imperative, they were to be on the lookout for extraneous words that might waste time, such as *please*. It was important to know exactly what you were going to say before any noises came out of you because you could get in trouble for *uhh* and *oh* and even *hmm*. If someone needed to clean a counter, they'd say, "Pass the squeegee," loud and clear, like a line in a play, but nothing more. At their various stations, Bristol and the other line cooks would dance around each other in a wordless ballet, and even in the silence, Bristol could tell which ones liked him and which ones were too bitter to like anyone. Bristol still didn't know any of his coworkers' names, not even the manager's. He supposed they were introduced once, but that had been years ago, and Bristol hadn't been paying attention, and to ask again would surely be considered a waste.

They were allowed to act as humans again just as soon as their shift was over and their cleaning was done and they were on their way home. But by that time, knowing his manager's name didn't seem important enough to ask. He hardly talked to anyone on the street or at the bus stop anyway. Bristol didn't have many friends apart from his sister. It seemed to him that his fellow unregs always had an excess of something within them—fear or anger or self-loathing. Mostly they were unhopeful creatures wrapped tightly up in themselves, which made sense to Bristol because society got along by pretending they didn't exist. Not that he was a saint. *We all have our ways of coping.*

What he preferred was to fade into the scenery and listen to the conversations of others, like a half-finished face in the background of some tableau, just witnessing the action. He liked to be inside his own head, to think of images to match the words he heard. Today, he took his seat on the bus behind two middle-aged women. He liked women's conversations the best. The one talking usually tried to be detailed, not leaving out important things like emotions, and the other one usually made those extra listening noises that peppered the talking nicely. He sat, looked out the window, and waited a moment for his ears to tune in.

"Relocate to where?" one of them said.

"They're saying out west, to the desert. There's lots of land out there."

"Then who would do—you know, the cooking and the cleaning and everything? We can't just get rid of them."

"There's an excess of Fives right now. Lots of people in higher tiers had their citizenship scores brought down, and that's the lowest they can drop."

"Hm!"

"But I've heard they're giving higher jobs to the Fives right now because the unregs have the menial labor market cornered and there are just so many Five jobs to go around."

"What?"

"Yes! My niece knows a Five who just got assigned as a bank teller!"

"No!"

"Yes! Just think—that poor girl has probably been taught to do customer service or repairs or whatever it is they teach the Fives, and just like that! Her future changes. They expect her to work with the interface bankbots, balance the amounts... It's a lot of responsibility! Surely she'd be more suited to a Five job."

"Surely!"

"But all the Five jobs are taken."

They must be Threes. Threes were always so afraid of anyone beneath them.

The second woman thought a moment. "What about the higher tiers? Won't this mean there'll be more work for us?"

"Oh, people will pitch in. I'd think this would give the robotics workers more incentive to improve their work to help us out. There's a rumor they're holding back now, trying not to take jobs away. Wouldn't be a problem if this goes through. It'll help us all financially too. Do you even *know* how much we're spending on the unregs?"

"Money that could be going back into the economy!" said the second.

"That's right."

The bus stopped and the ladies scuffled off, both stopping to thank the driver. How much of what they said was true? Probably the bit about robotics slowing to accommodate jobs. A human driving this bus was proof of that. *Don't worry about it too much.* Talk like this came up every now and then, saving resources and such. But less than fifty years ago, people deemed unfit to procreate were sterilized, and everyone else was forced to have only one child. Wasn't it enough? The unregs weren't hurting anyone, and if it helped the Fives to let them drive instead of upgrading the busses, why couldn't they just do that?

A picture began in his mind's eye, as if it had always existed and someone were just blowing dust off the surface. The face of a watch lying on the ground. The screen showed the middle of some transaction. A hand cupped it from underneath, with the palm up and the fingers curling in, attached to a crushed body below. He took out his notebook and sketched it.

"Oi!"

Bristol looked up. He was the only one still on the bus.

The driver looked at him through the rearview. "Missir stop?"

Bristol threw his notebook and pencil into his backpack. "Oh...yeah."

"Where were you supposed to get off?"

"Larkin Station."

The driver shook his head. "You'll never make it back there before curfew." The bus gave a sudden exhale. "I've got my scooter. I'll take you. I'm going that way anyway."

Moments later, Bristol hung on to a bar behind his seat as the scooter flew through the quickly emptying streets. He'd never been on a scooter before but couldn't imagine never going on one again. He should try to convince Denver to buy one. The two of them could ride like this every night...

Except they couldn't, he remembered. In a few days she'd be married, and he'd be the only one sleeping in the little bedroom with the one loose bar at the window. And then there was the problem of this graffiti arrest... Suppose it wasn't over? *Just stop. Just enjoy this ride.*

"Y'smell like onions!" shouted the driver over his shoulder.

"It's garlic. I'm a cook."

Usually this admission about his profession inspired some sort of credence. Bristol liked his day job well enough and there was usually some confidence in his voice on the rare occasions he told other people. But this driver, casually in control of this soaring metal beast, only nodded. Bristol got the impression he knew who he was too, and he was proud of it.

All too soon, they halted in front of Bristol's building.

Bristol stuck out his hand. "Thanks very much."

The driver took it and shook. "No problem, man. By the way, those bushes in front of your building...they ever burn?"

"What?"

"Ever see any burning bushes?" He looked at Bristol like he knew something, expected something.

"I don't know what you're talking about."

The driver frowned. "Stupid joke. Anyway, you're welcome."

He sped off, leaving Bristol standing there, unable to decide if he was more curious to know more or relieved he didn't.

CHAPTER EIGHT

ON MONDAY MORNING, SAMARA MET HER NEW BOSS. WARDEN Paul was a tall woman made even taller with the help of her shiny black stilettos. Her uniform, pressed to perfection, looked as if it had grown on her, and she seemed the type to keep an identical one in her drawer for sleeping. Though Samara had diligently practiced good posture the entire bus ride over, she shrank in the presence of this glistening giant. Warden Paul had barely laid eyes on Samara when she gestured for her to follow and clacked down the hall and into the cafeteria past the boys eating their lunches. Silence grew in waves as she made her way to the front. She snapped her heels together, drew her hands behind her back, and surveyed the room. Yes, they were all listening. She smiled with her square teeth but not her eyes.

"Inmates!"

A droning chorus answered, "Yes, Warden Paul."

She smiled wider to a frightening effect. "Answer crispier! Inmates!"

"Yes, Warden Paul!"

"That's better. We will now practice our new meal routine. From now on, you will have one minute to eat your food as quickly as you

can. Then you will have twenty seconds of rest. During the rest, you
are not to touch any food or drink. Your hands will be in your lap.
You will have three rounds of this, and then you will clean up and be
dismissed for work. We will do this because it is fun. Now, how long
will you have to eat your food?" She paused. "Nelson!"

"One minute, three times."

"Yes. How long will you have to rest? Jordan!"

"Twenty seconds, three times."

"And why are we doing this? Kopecky!"

Kopecky mumbled, shoulders hunched into his ears.

"Loud and proud, Kopecky."

His eyes turned upward. "Because it's fun."

"Because it is fun! Practice first when I say begin."

The Kopecky boy glanced toward a younger kid with boxy blue
glasses. He looked oddly familiar; where had she seen his face
before?

"Begin!"

Frantic eating ensued. The sloshes and smacks of openmouthed
chewing and gasps for air filled the hall. The sounds knitted together
with the smells of overcooked rice, boiled asparagus, and fried tofu,
daring Samara to gag in front of Warden Paul. Paul herself calmly
watched, totally unaffected, even relaxed in her wide-legged stance
of authority.

After the practice round, the whole ordeal was complete in four
minutes flat. At the scream of a whistle, the boys—some of them
wiping thin streams of vomit from their mouths—formed single-file
lines. Once the room was clear, Paul turned to Samara with a self-
satisfied smirk.

"From thirty minutes to four. Today our operation just became
thirteen percent more efficient."

"That's very—"

"Yes, Miss Shepherd, it's just the way things are done around
here. We are efficient with our resources. Efficient with money,
efficient with time, though that's just really money in disguise. When
I first arrived twenty years ago, this place was underperforming. I

turned it around." Her eyes flashed to Samara, this time in a true smile. "Want to know the secret?"

Samara wanted to say yes, but by the time she'd opened her mouth, Paul was already talking.

"Push until they break. Once they do, you'll know to back off a little. But until they do, don't be afraid to discover what's possible." She walked back toward her office so quickly that Samara had to trot along after her. "When one of them chokes, we'll know we've gone too far. We'll try a revised schedule next week to allow for shorter breaks and see what happens. You've got to get buy-in from them, though, for it to work. Just tell them they'll enjoy it." She shook her head. "Mealtimes! Why didn't I think of shaving off minutes there?"

"How *did* you think of it, Warden?"

Paul snorted. "It wasn't me at all, if you must know. It was an inmate."

"They come to you with ideas?"

"They don't have ideas. We simply observed the behavior of one of them. He's in for an incurable mental condition, so it comes as no surprise he was acting funny. I simply noticed he was logging more hours in the work room and asked myself *why*. That's really the attitude you need to get things done. Always keep growing."

"A growth mindset," said Samara.

"Yes, good, whatever you'd like to call it." Paul stopped behind her enormous desk. Her face glowed in the anemic light reflecting off the glossy surface. "We're so glad you're here, Miss Shepherd. I think you'll find we are truly doing good...for the inmates and for society. Do you have any questions?"

"I do. Are the boys paid for their work? For once they get out?"

"In the form of room and board, they are paid generously. The beds are comfortable and they receive a hot meal three times a day. Money, no, but they have no need for it."

"What about when they get out?"

"They'll find jobs at that time. Their time here is about serving society."

Samara shifted on her feet. "What have they done, mostly? I'm interested to know what problems to expect."

"Most of them have done nothing yet. But behavior reports suggest that they're *inclined* toward crime, and so most of them are here as a preventative measure."

In prison with no crime committed? It sounded like an idea her mother would love. Then Samara remembered her mother was far away, picking blueberries.

Warden Paul narrowed her eyes and sat down. "It may seem cruel, but the reports are very reliable. Surely you wouldn't want to risk any actual crimes taking place?"

Samara also took a seat. "No, of course not. Why didn't I know about this before?"

"They always have some story they tell the public. Sometimes it's to hide the fact the police can't manage to locate a criminal themselves!"

Samara thought a moment. A few years ago, this would have shocked her, but she was more grown-up now. More worldly. If they were certain the inmates would eventually have a reason for being locked away, why shouldn't society be protected from them? And anyway, even if she thought differently, things were different now. Samara had a well-paying job, and her mother was in the country picking berries. If Samara wanted to see her in the next five years, she'd have to keep working here to save her money for the fine. This was not a time for nobility.

"That's very smart," she said.

"Yes, the public loves a good capture. We've had one recent case of that. A boy was sent here to cover for a graffiti problem. He suffers from mental illness and needed a reason to be removed from the outside world, and the police needed a conclusion. Necessary for calming the public. Everybody wins." She raised her watch and projected some charts onto her desk. "I don't have to remind you that you've signed confidentiality agreements, Miss Shepherd."

"Of course. I can see how this might look to outsiders."

"Thank you, dear. I will observe your first lesson at eight o'clock tomorrow. Goodbye for now."

Samara stood and turned toward the door. Her fingertips paused on the gleaming knob. She turned back. "One more question. The boy with the incurable mental illness, what's wrong with him exactly?"

Paul waved her hand at the hologram, summoning a mug shot of the boy with the blue glasses. "A history of nonreliable personal governance. He tends to make decisions based on his own ideas of what is right or wrong."

"Oh. Yes." Samara bit her lip. "And...that's a problem big enough for prison?"

Paul lowered her chin. "Yes, it is. Who knows what his ideas of right and wrong are? What if he decided to break a rule because he decided it wasn't right? Most of us make decisions based on reward or punishment. When one person doesn't do that, they threaten to break the harmony we're all accustomed to living with. That one has some deeper problems as well—everyone expects children to be a bit awkward, but for the children raised in higher tiers, there is less leniency. And this one is as awkward as they come. Something may have gone wrong with his genetics." She did her weird teeth-only smile again. "Miss Shepherd, I'm *glad* you're asking these questions. Thank you for the opportunity to answer them! You'll do very well here."

But Samara's focus was back on the mug shot. She finally realized where she'd seen him before—in her own apartment, in front of the hall window where she stood to admire the paintings. She'd been looking at that wall transform through her window for five years. That graffiti would be back soon, though Jude would not. Who else would they lock up under false pretenses in the name of order? Would they ever catch the real artist, or was it more convenient to let him paint?

Back at home, Samara's dad had an illegal glass of vodka and some interesting news. "I heard from your mother today."

Samara dropped her heavy bag to the floor but felt no relief in her shoulder. "How is she?"

One corner of his mouth rose. "She's fine. She's got a tan."

"So what's wrong?"

"Who says anything's wrong?"

"You can tell me."

Her father took a swig. "She's very close to a place she shouldn't be. Sometimes people run away from the city for one reason or another. No watches, no money or food or even a map to know where they're going. Anyway, the farm she's on is close to one of these...checkpoints, I guess you could call it. Safe houses, along the route to wherever they go."

Samara watched him. "How does she know?"

"She saw a couple of people run and hide right near the blueberry bushes. And then she thinks she saw someone come get them. They went in the direction of this house that's close to her apartment." He shook his head. "Honestly, if they know she even saw them, her score could get docked..."

"Don't worry. She'll be home soon." She took his almost-empty glass and turned it over in the sink. "I have a good feeling about this job."

CHAPTER NINE

DENVER DIDN'T QUITE KNOW WHY SHE HADN'T TOLD BRISTOL about their real father yet. Her relationship with her mother had turned icy, and she could certainly use an ally. And yet it wasn't that she was angry exactly, more like appalled at the stupidity of the woman Denver had always admired for her strength and intelligence. *You can't trust anyone.*

Besides that, she needed to be strong for Bristol. Very shortly, she'd be in a new home with a new husband while Bristol would be stuck here with a woman who thought having two children with a lover was a good idea. A part of her wished she hadn't applied for marriage at all. Bristol certainly needed her more than her mystery husband did. And even if that weren't true, Bristol was the one she already had a responsibility to. Bristol was the one who had to give up the one thing he loved—his art—to protect himself and Mom. There were so many people in the world—not as many as before the uprising, but still millions—that you really had to conserve your kindness. You had to draw a circle around those you loved most and not give a damn about what happened to anyone outside it. Why, then, did she feel the need to expand that circle to include a husband and his family and a child of her own? Everyone except

Fives were required to try, at least, for one baby. Metrics would know if they didn't try, or if she tried to sabotage their efforts by withholding sex. She wondered, briefly, if the reason she'd applied for marriage was to elevate her own social status. She groaned and brought her wrist to her eyes. Soon, she was scrolling through her favorite shopping app, on the hunt for the perfect pair of blue heels for the wedding.

She'd been pleased when she saw Stephen's height—six foot one —a full five inches taller than she was. It meant she could wear heels, but also that even though she was marrying down a tier, the Office of Domestic Affairs still gave her a reasonably good assignment. Given their measurements, their child would probably inherit some height as well.

She scrolled through the same shoe pictures a few times, and then she sighed and checked the time. Checked the weather. There was a message from Mom asking when Denver would be home today, but she didn't reply.

"Hey, Den?" Her coworker, Felicia, was peeking over the cubicle wall.

"Hey, what's up?"

"Wanna get an energy shot?"

Under the desk, Denver's feet slid into her shoes. She pushed herself away. "Sure."

With their arms crossed, Denver and Felicia hustled out of the chilly office. They walked outside, where Denver immediately relaxed, as if she were a puppet and someone had released her strings. The energy shot kiosk was just a short walk through the courtyard, but both girls took lazy strides, savoring the warm air and the smell of fresh-cut grass.

"So I heard you got your letter," Felicia said.

Denver looked down at the paved walking path winding them around the greenery. "I did."

"So did I."

Denver looked up at Felicia, whose face was fixed on the walkway. "I thought they told you they couldn't pair you!"

"I guess someone got their score docked! I don't know what happened, but I'm grateful. Anyway, my letter came yesterday."

"And?"

"He's perfect. I think. He's in your class, Denver. He's going to be an architect too."

"Maybe I know him. What's his name?"

"Thatcher."

It was a stupid question to ask. "Actually, I don't know anyone's names. We're not allowed to talk in those classes."

"Well, he's handsome. Here's a picture." Felicia held out her arm. She plopped her right elbow on the bar when they reached the kiosk and leaned toward the cashier. "Two shots, please." She turned to Denver. "Green?"

Denver didn't take her eyes off her friend's watch. "Green."

This Thatcher was handsome in an old-fashioned, rugged way. A Three, of course, with cool outdoorsy interests like cycling and trail running. Denver couldn't see Felicia keeping up with him in the woods, with sweat tracks down her face and dirt on her clothes. This was just the sort of thing Denver had been hoping for in a spouse assignment—someone who could introduce her to new things, who could turn her into a new version of herself. Denver thought of her own assignment and her stomach turned.

"Here, Den."

"Thanks." She took the little green bottle, upturned it to empty the contents into her mouth, and handed it back to the cashier.

"Well, back to work. Just an hour to go!"

Denver scoffed. "Just an hour more of data entry. Then classes all afternoon."

"That's what I meant. Is something wrong?"

"No." *Yes.* "Nothing's wrong." *Yes, it is. I am better than you at data entry. Better at school. I have better test scores. We're in the same tier. Yet you get a better spouse than me, a better life than me. It's not fair.*

Felicia shivered. "Whew, I feel it now."

"So do I." Denver did feel the usual surge of adrenaline that came with the energy shots, but it was different this time, too jittery. She had to get back inside before she said something she'd regret.

Thankfully, the conversation turned away from grooms and toward wedding attire and they went back to chatting happily until they stepped back into the frigid office. Once inside her cubical again, Denver placed her hands on the keyboard, this time able to feel the blood pulsing in her fingertips. *Shake it off.* She projected a report next to the computer screen and typed. She read and wrote without understanding.

As her fingers worked, her mind wandered. Back to Felicia and Thatcher and Stephen and the injustice of it all and then to the awful place minds go when they're upset—shame.

She was forced back to a place she'd often tried to forget. The neighborhood playground. School had been let out for a break, and on the first day of a four-day holiday, she'd been allowed to play with other kids. The sun was setting, but ten-year-old Denver had no intention of going back inside. She was nursing an impending friendship with a few other kids. She chased them around the playground, basking in this rare inclusion, feeling part of the group.

Bristol walked to the edge of the playground. "Denver! Mom says come home!"

Denver frowned and kept running.

"*Denver!* Mom says…"

One of the boys leered down at Bristol from the top of the slide. "*Denver! Denver!*" His tone was two registers above Bristol's. "Why should she care what your mom says, anyway? You cousins or something?"

Don't tell them.

"She's my sister!"

Denver grasped a platform with straight arms. She let her lower body go limp and dunked her head down onto her chest at the word *sister*.

"Oooh!" the other boy said. "Denver, your mom had two kids?"

"That means she did it twice!"

Their laughter resounded from the tubes of plastic and metal. Denver's feet found the soft ground and she marched over to Bristol.

"Just go away! You're embarrassing both of us."

"But—"

"Go away!"

Bristol turned and ran. It wasn't until he was at least a block away that Denver heard applause from behind. The other kids had forgotten about humiliating Denver. They gazed down at her with admiration, loudly celebrating her cruelty.

She didn't remember anything else. Did she ever apologize to Bristol for that day? Was it too late to tell him she was sorry?

Denver looked up at the screen and found that the computer had input the addresses into the zip code box. She huffed and fixed it. Then she realized it had done the same thing on all the addresses.

This entire marriage business was just too distracting. It was all Mom's idea, anyway, and Denver was a fool to have listened. It had been two days since she had received her assignment and she couldn't stand the way it was already dragging her down. The prospect of fifty years of boredom and indignity was unbearable.

That's it.

She was just going to have to get out of it.

CHAPTER TEN

JUDE'S FAVORITE PART OF PRISON WAS SCHOOL.

He was finally the smart kid. Out in the real world, his schoolwork was challenging, and wrong answers meant punishment. Jude preferred to think over the questions, to rule out all wrong answers completely to avoid punishments, but that cost him time. His education managers couldn't bear giving him time. They'd rather have wrong answers.

Miss Shepherd, on the other hand, seemed thrilled by all guesses, correct or incorrect. Though she was just teaching basic phonetics, she lit up the room when someone spelled *watch* with an *sh* instead of a *ch*, and she prodded the boy to explain why he made that choice. But it wasn't public shaming; it was raw curiosity.

He got the courage to talk to her one day while she had recess duty. Jude was terrible at all the games the boys played, so he usually hung back and watched, mostly with Kopecky. On the day Kopecky had a hearing, he tiptoed closer and closer to Miss Shepherd until she said, "Hello there."

"Hello. I'm Jude."

"I know who you are, Jude Reeder. That's a good name for you. You are a good reader."

"I've been reading for a long time."

"You were a Two."

Jude's head jolted up. "How did you know that?"

"I've seen your record." Her words, Jude noticed, didn't exactly match her expression; the words were glib, but her face had turned away from the other boys completely, her eyes focused in just on Jude. Feeling a blush begin, he turned his sights to the boys she was supposed to be watching. "I just wanted to tell you that I like the way you teach. I like how you ask us to think about why we got the wrong answer. I'll keep doing that when I get back to my Two school. I wanted to tell you now, because I'm sure I'll be leaving here soon." He turned back to her, still a little unnerved to have her full attention. "I'm innocent."

He assumed she'd thank him and tell him to run off and play, but she surprised him again, with two words as soft as his bed at home.

"I know."

Jude was free, and his parents had come to collect him with a little brother in his mother's arms. They were proud of him for enduring prison, for making his mark while he was here to improve efficiency, and for alerting the staff to Mr. Richards's terrible mistake. Mr. Richards was there too, and he was awfully sorry for any trouble he'd caused. At that point in the dream, Jude was holding his brother, marveling over his little fingers and toes, and he was happy to forgive and forget.

Let bygones be bygones, he said, but they couldn't hear him. He said it louder.

They cupped their hands to their ears. *What?*

He said it again, louder.

He woke himself when he realized he was talking in his sleep. He sighed and looked at the room. A little white cell with three sets of white-painted bunk beds, each with an adolescent-shaped lump beneath the white sheets. By the look of the sun, it was nearly time to get up anyway; soon, the lights would flash on and the Metrics anthem would blare from the loudspeakers to signal wake-up time. After that, the sheet of glass that served as the fourth wall would lift from the floor and the guards would come in to check for cleanliness and escort them to breakfast. Jude was glad he'd woken up today his way; he swung his feet onto the floor and made his bed.

Although they'd all been taught from the time they were very young to make the bed the same way, most children and adults reverted to the shortcut, unless they were due for a check-in from Metrics. Jude had stayed true to the bed-making routine as it was originally taught, and today it served him well. In the center of the bed between the mattress and the iron frame was a small bag of white powder.

He had never seen any actual drugs before, so he would have liked the chance to pick the bag up and sniff it to be sure it wasn't laundry detergent or sugar or something else strange and innocent, but he wasn't going to get that chance. The other boys would be waking up any moment, and the early morning sun was already dampening the room. *Think. Focus. Think.* The time to figure out the details—who, when, and why—would have to wait. He thought briefly of tossing it in the center of the room and taking the chance that nobody—or all six of them—would be blamed. But he thought of Kopecky, sleeping soundly in the bunk above him, and knew he couldn't be the cause of him going eight days without food again. Anyway, the cameras were set off by sensors; as long as Jude stayed beside his bed, he was hidden—he hoped—but if he threw the bag, the cameras would turn on to reveal five sleeping bystanders and Jude standing and looking very guilty. That meant flushing the bag down the little stainless steel toilet was out too, as he'd have to cross the room to get to it. The sun was rising quickly. *Think.*

Through the morning calm came the Warden's voice over the loudspeaker: "Good morning, boys. Surprise inspection today."

No time. Jude's knees buckled, so he crouched next to his bed with the bag still in his hand. Suddenly, as if his body acted of its own will, he stuffed the bag inside one of his socks. The other boys were stirring now, making halfhearted noises of protest as they rose. Jude swallowed some hot saliva, shivered, and ran his hand over his ashen-colored arm. The hair on it stood stiff. Black spots formed over the other boys stuffing sheets into the corners of their beds.

Kopeckey eyed him. "You okay, buddy?"

"Me?" Even as he said it, he began to feel better. "Yeah." The bag slipped. Maybe if he was able to get it under the arch of his foot, he'd be able to pull it off.

The glass lowered. The Warden herself stepped over the crack in the floor and stood tall in the center, encircled by the sleepy boys. Two guards, both young women wearing makeup, which made their faces look sculpted and perfect, stood just behind her. Ms. Shepherd stood behind them, as if to watch and learn how to do inspections. Paul inhaled fully and looked them over with a smile.

"Well," she said. "Good morning, boys."

Everyone except Jude returned the greeting. Jude was still concentrating hard on wiggling the bag under his foot.

"Again, more cheerful! Good morning, boys!"

Jude snapped his feet together as if he were standing at attention. This time he joined in. "Good morning, Warden!"

"That will have to do. Let's not waste time; we have received a tip that someone in the building is hiding something. Naughty, naughty. Fox boys are treated very well, and if you've decided you want something we cannot offer, we feel it would be best if you were relocated."

From the corner of his eye, Jude saw Kopeckey shudder.

"Prepare for a pat down on your marks," she said.

Jude was already standing on his mark—the place on the floor marked with a small black dot. They were required to stand here during inspections to ensure they were just the right distance apart from their beds and each other, so they could not help hide anything. His stomach churned.

"Begin!"

They went to Kopecky's bed first. The guards ruffled the bedclothes, took the pillowcase off and tossed it on the floor, and peeked inside his shoes under the bed. The inspection took less than ten seconds, less time than it took them to check that their beds were made correctly during daily inspection. One guard lazily ran her hand up and down Kopecky's sides. Then she took a step back. Jude began to suspect something horrible. "Clean," one said to the warden.

They moved to the next two beds and boys in line, declaring them clean in even less time than they'd taken with Kopecky. The warden's eyes turned hungrily to the next boy. Jude forced himself to meet her gaze as the guards began to untuck his sheets.

"Ladies, allow me." Warden Paul pounced on Jude's bed and vigorously snatched the sheet away from the mattress. "Remember, the tip we received was quite serious, and we mustn't stop until we find what we're looking for. And we *will* find it!"

Unable to help herself, she flipped the mattress onto the floor and stared at the empty bed frame.

She stood there staring for several seconds. Blinking, she rushed to the other side and rifled through the bedclothes again, running her hand up and down the mattress several times. Everyone in the cell was staring at her now. All over his body, Jude's skin was white-hot and beading with sweat.

The warden stopped and sharply turned her head toward his mark. Her voice was a hiss. "Search him."

The guards, now compelled to follow their boss's example, flung their arms at Jude's body, beating their hands against his rib cage, hips, groin, legs, and, inciting an involuntary gag, his ankles. Jude pushed the floor away with his feet, standing a little taller on the bag.

"Clean," said one guard, with a little less conviction than she'd declared the previous three boys.

"May I?" asked Paul, and began her own pat down. She patted, rubbed, and slid her hands all over Jude. When she was still unable to find what she was looking for, she gave the back of his head a clean slap. Jude fought for control to stay upright. If he passed out, it was all over for him; the legal system would do its job and keep him behind bars forever.

Warden Paul leaned in very close to his face. "Perhaps one of our friends has swallowed the contraband."

At that very moment, that the contents of Jude's stomach escaped his body and landed with a terrible squelch onto the floor, and most unfortunately, on Warden Paul's shiny black pumps. No one moved for a second, and Jude found himself feeling relieved in spite of the situation he was still in.

One of the guards allowed a smile to creep across her face. "Well, I think we can rule that one out."

Paul closed her eyes and exhaled. "The tip we received indicated that the contraband was in this cell, number sixty-five. I trust that you can locate it. The boys must learn that they cannot hide."

She walked out of the cell. The sound of squishing shoes could be heard all the way down the hall.

Jude and his cellmates survived the nearly two hours they were forced to stand on their marks. After the guards left their cell and cleared them to continue on to their work assignments, he could feel the eyes of the five other boys on him.

Later, one of them asked, "What did you do?"

"Nothing!"

"I'm Brown, by the way." The boy named Brown stuck out his hand, and Jude shook it warily. "Why are they blaming you?"

"I don't know!" Was this how you lied? Jude had never told a lie before. He'd never had a reason until today.

"You can tell us!"

"Maybe you didn't hear," said Kopecky. "He said he didn't know."

Jude's head was spinning again, and there was nothing in his stomach this time to provide him any respite. "I didn't do anything to deserve coming here, and I'm not doing anything wrong while I'm here. I'm getting out. I'm not like you."

The next day, Jude's jaw was still sore from Brown's fist, and Kopecky refused to speak to him.

And he still had the bag—the plastic ever threatening to break from his uncontrollable twisting and prodding—in his pocket.

CHAPTER ELEVEN

BRISTOL STUCK A NEW STENCIL TO THE WALL AND OPENED HIS CAN of yellow. He had never been caught because it was easy to discern whether the presence behind him was friend or foe.

It was always a friend. If he heard a voice behind him, without having heard them coming, they were just another unreg, out roaming the night. The cameras all had their ranges, and it wasn't difficult to learn how to stay on the outskirts of them. The police always made a racket in their cars, which, despite quietness being a major component of their design, gave little low whistles that could be heard from blocks away. The police never learned how to step without making the gravel crunch beneath their feet or slow their breathing until their bodies were almost truly still. The unregistered lived silent lives.

Most of them were looking for Drift. Bristol had done his fair share of the stuff, but he liked creating graffiti better, and he couldn't concentrate on making things—or anything else—when he was on it. Maybe the problem was that he'd never had friends to share it with. He was always alone on his trips, sprawled on his bed like a beached starfish. He was separate from his body and his mind and could observe his thoughts drifting through his mind as easily as he could watch clouds pass in the sky. Always, at least one of those thoughts was a hope that Denver would think he was just sleeping if she happened to wake up and see him. Coming out of the trance in the morning was heartbreaking. The following day would pass with no sleep and no food—what was the point?—and there'd be nothing to savor or delight or comfort until that evening, when he held the white powder in his palm again, anticipating the next few hours of oblivion. He'd wasted two years of early adolescence like this. A part of him bought into the common unregistered philosophy: life doesn't matter. You may as well spend your time feeling good, or at least not feeling bad.

Bristol wasn't ready to turn down that philosophy entirely yet. And yes, he realized he'd probably just traded one drug for another, because drawing made him feel good, and so did watching people look at what he'd done, and so did listening for police cars while he worked. But though all signs pointed to the meaninglessness of his life, something else made him want to believe otherwise. He didn't want to think about it too hard. He wanted to paint about it. He inhaled the damp night air and the paint and felt his lungs swell. He was aware of his heartbeat. *I am. I am. I am.*

There were days where he was glad his previous fantasy about being registered and working as an assigned Artist would never come to be. It used to make him so angry, so hopeless, so prone to sniffing powder and just watching thoughts swirl thorough his mind. Now, it seemed such a silly thing that Metrics would ask someone with pictures for thoughts to make something pretty for a park, or a courthouse, or a rich person's house. He might as well be a bricklayer, just following the plans. If that would have been his job anyway, why not chop vegetables for a living?

Bristol stepped back and observed his painting. He should have moved the stencil down a quarter of an inch to make the wings appear more symmetrical, but besides that, he was satisfied. It was a small image, one he hoped wouldn't attract too much attention so people would have the chance to look before it was destroyed. On the side of the public library, there was now a little blue book burning on the brick wall. Out of the flames, a young butterfly flew toward one of the barred windows. Bristol had seen an old movie about a library. If the movie was to be trusted, libraries used to house tens of thousands of books, not hundreds of computers in individual plastic stalls. Maybe his picture would spark some recognition in a kindly old librarian. Maybe she would let it stay.

Don't get emotionally attached, Denver would say.

Bristol gathered his supplies and thought of his sister. He'd never had to worry about her before. It was a strange change, ever since that letter came. When her appeal to leave her impending marriage contract was denied, she had responded, as Bristol expected she would, with more research and a lengthy letter. She strutted around for a day, positive they'd reconsider. But they didn't, and now it looked like Denver really would have to marry the Four. She knew it and grew more depressed. For a few days after that, she didn't shower. Bristol knew the kinder thing would have been to offer to find her some Drift, but he lacked the courage to watch his sister go through that.

"The worst part of it," Denver had said with puffy eyes and a set jaw, "is that I know the woman who keeps denying my appeals. I bet she doesn't even know I work in her office." She wiped a tear with the back of her hand. "Mrs. *A. A.* thinks she's too important to go by a real name. She needs more *privacy*."

The wheels in Bristol's mind had turned then. "Does she ever work late?"

Denver had snorted. "Always. Almost every night. She's always going on about how much she has to do and how she was the last one at the office at night and the first there in the morning. It's sick."

The memory of her words echoed in his mind as he walked away from the butterfly.

———

Getting an official Metrics janitor's uniform was a little tricky. Bristol had gone to Denver's office on his day off to make friends with the cleaning staff there and ask for this favor. He approached one of the janitors, a woman named Jelani, whom he discovered had just had a baby one week ago, and offered to draw a portrait of them together in exchange for this small favor. Bristol had brought his notebook with him and did a quick sketch to give her a sample of his work. A few minutes later, he handed her an honest sketch of her grooved face, stringy hair, and something in her eyes that looked like daring. Fifteen minutes later, he was dressed no differently than the other unregs in the building. She'd given him a uniform, and he put it on over his clothes until he looked like he belonged with the rest of the staff. The only difference in his appearance might have been his running shoes, but he was not taking those off.

Mrs. A. A. worked on the thirteenth floor, like Denver, and though Bristol could just make up a name for her, he thought it would be better if he actually knew it. He didn't expect it to work, but he approached the reception desk in his janitor's uniform.

"Excuse me?"

The security guard at the reception desk sighed deeply, clearly to indicate that Bristol was interrupting something. He lowered his watch away from his face. "Yes?"

"I'm supposed to go do Mrs. A. A.'s office. But there are two Mrs. A. A.s."

The man's mouth was still in a sour shape, but he set up a hologram on his desk. "I only see one here. Allison Ansberry? Works at the Department of Domestic Affairs?"

"Okay. Where's that?"

"Thirteenth floor."

"Thank you."

Amazed at the success despite the simplicity of this plan, Bristol stepped onto the elevator armed with everything he needed to bring a drop of justice to Denver's life.

When the elevator doors opened, he walked around the office looking at the names on the doors: Mr. P. W., Mrs. R. B., Ms. K. H. People were rushing around everywhere talking into their watches or carrying stacks of paper. No one gave him a second glance even though he carried no cleaning supplies and his sneakers made little squawks as he walked. He congratulated himself on coming when so many people were around, but he hadn't planned that. He couldn't see Denver anywhere, but he was sure he'd see her—and more importantly, that she'd see him—just as soon as the action started.

When he arrived at Mrs. A. A.'s door, he was also delighted to see that several men and women were in her office, discussing something that required the use of pie chart projections. He guessed she was the one behind the desk. She was probably fifty years old, but had makeup tattooed on her lifted face to make her look at least twenty years younger. He circled the hallway one last time to plan his escape route. Looked like a bit of a hike to the stairwell, but it didn't matter. *Talk fast.*

He puffed up his chest, marched straight over to Mrs. A. A.'s door, and threw it open.

"Allison!"

The people inside gaped at him. He stood in the doorway and started straight at her as convincingly as he could.

"Allison, it's no use. It's been good, baby, but it's over!"

The woman behind the desk stood slowly and opened her mouth, but he couldn't tell if she was outraged yet or just very confused. In his peripherals, he saw heads popping out of offices. He kept talking.

"I know what you're going to say, and no! I can't go on! It's not fair to your husband!"

Mrs. A. A. flushed crimson as the people in her office looked at her for a response. "I...I don't know who you are!" she said and looked around at the people sitting on the couch. "I don't know who this person is!"

Bristol would have felt sorry for her if it hadn't been for the way she'd treated Denver—choosing to think of Denver as a slice of a pie in her charts and not as a living, breathing person. Mrs. A. A. deserved a reminder that everyone is an individual capable of emotion, even she.

"You always said you'd deny it, Allison. Maybe this was the wrong way to do this. But I won't be back tonight. You'll have to go back to your husband if you want your kicks."

"I don't know you!" Mrs. A. A. shrieked, and Bristol decided she'd had enough. *Time to go.*

He sprinted down the hallway toward the stairwell. Over his shoulder, he shouted, "I'll always have fond memories of that couch!"

He imagined her seated colleagues jumping to their feet with disgusted expressions and laughed. A crowd formed in the hall, but everyone was too shocked to know what to do. Surely none of their emergency drills accounted for a janitor publicly breaking off an affair with the boss, so the employees must have felt paralyzed. Bristol took advantage and ran as fast as he could before the spell could be broken. Sure enough, he had a brief glimpse of Denver. Her incredulous smile made her stand out from the dumbstruck faces around her. Bristol looked forward to laughing with her later, but for now he just ran, down the stairs, past the security guard at the front, and out into the street, feeling like a little kid's picture of a hero.

CHAPTER TWELVE

THERE WAS BLOOD ON SAMARA'S SHEETS.

She'd noticed the dampness right after she put her feet on the floor and felt shocked. Had she wet the bed, like a toddler? Even with no one to see, she burned with shame until she saw the red smear on the cheap plastic white sheet. *What happened?* She checked her body, but the only place it could have come from seemed to be inside her. There was a puddle in her underwear, and her inner thighs were sticky.

Somehow it felt wrong to tell Dad, but she had to tell someone. She was dying! There was no other possible explanation. She didn't know how long she'd be able to function like this, but it couldn't last long. She wished her mother were here.

She called The Public Medline and listened to a robotic voice present the menu of options. Was she a patient? A provider? A caregiver? Did she need to know the hours of operation? Directions to the office? Did she have questions about any injections (*Get all of your injections on time, every time!* the voice warned). She tried to slow her breath so as not to panic.

"Please state your emergency," the robot's voice said.

"I'm bleeding from inside. It's coming out of my..." She didn't know what to call it. All she knew were slang terms, and those didn't feel like the right words to say on The Medline.

"When was the date of your last focus injection?"

What does that have to do with it? "May 6," Samara answered.

"Please report to your school or workplace for an immediate injection. Bleeding will cease shortly thereafter. Thank you for calling The Public Medline, a service of your Worldwide Metric Government."

She tapped her watch to end the call and breathed a sigh of relief. Come to think of it, she was due for another injection. It had been such a busy time that she'd forgotten all about them. Fox County Detention Center must have too. *So that's what the medicine's really for.* She'd always thought it just helped her think more clearly.

She cleaned herself and packed a change of underwear in her bag in case it happened again before she got her shot.

When she arrived at work, she walked straight to the guard behind the front door and asked how soon she'd be able to get an injection. The guard, a young woman about her age, looked striking in her tight navy jumpsuit with gold trim.

"We don't get those here," she told Samara. "Are you bleeding? The employee locker room has pads. Just go in and look in the cabinet." The guard's watch began to blink with a yellow light. "Excuse me," she said and answered a phone call.

Samara went to the locker room. Inside the cabinet were pillow-like tissues that, once unwrapped, were sticky on one side. She puzzled over them for a moment, but it didn't take her long to realize what they were for. She noticed dampness and found that her underwear was once again soaked in blood. Her hands shook as she changed into her new pair and placed the pad on them. How long would this continue?

At work, she was distracted. She felt a little funny, but she was unquestionably still able to perform her duties. Halfway through the day, she was mortified to see that she needed another pad, as the first one had been saturated. She placed the first one in her bag with her red-stained underwear. She didn't know what to do with either, but she'd figure it out later.

On her way home, she sat on the back row of the bus to conduct some searches on her watch in private. All of the information listed seemed to be censored. If she was a medical professional, the tiny hologram projected on her lap read, she'd be able to put in her number and bypass the security page. She turned off her watch with a huff, causing the hologram to disappear, and rested her head back on the seat. She grimaced and massaged her stomach. All this worry seemed to be making her sick.

At her stop, she stood and stepped off, eager to get home.

"Hey!" A voice came from the street. "Samara!"

Irritation rang through Samara's whole being until she saw that the person walking toward her was Bristol. The sight of him made her think of the brick wall outside her window, which, of course, had a new image on it.

"Hi. Bristol, right?"

"Yep." Bristol's smile was wide and warm.

"Oh. I didn't know if that was your real name or not. You also told me last time that you made soup," she said, eying his janitor's uniform.

"I did—I do. I borrowed this."

"Quite a fashion statement."

"No, just something stupid for my...friend." He told her about his friend and her misery, and then recounted his adventure in the Department of Domestic Affairs. As he talked, Samara's stomach pain seemed further away, and when he got to the part about breaking it off with Mrs. A. A., Samara laughed for the first time all day.

"I mean, it's not *really* funny. You could have been caught, and then you'd be in real trouble," she said, though her cheeks were still high on her face. "I wish I had someone to do things like that for me."

"Well, what do you need? I'm a vigilante in a one-man justice club. At your service."

She laughed again, shook her head, and looked down at her watch. Not flashing. "Come with me."

She took him to the fire escape outside her building. While Bristol waited on the street below, Samara climbed to the second floor, unhinged her watch, and stashed it in her bag.

"Won't your dad find it?" Bristol asked.

She climbed back down and readjusted her skirt. "No, he won't. My dad's probably drunk already. I don't want you to think any less of him, though. He just misses my mom."

"But he's still got you."

"I don't want to talk about this. I want to show you something."

She pointed toward the wall covered in fresh plastic. They dove under it and plunged themselves into a world of blue light. On the wall, there was a small, simple painting of a bowl of fruit. Samara was disappointed to see Bristol shrink at the sight of it.

"I thought you'd think...well, I think it's funny."

"What?"

"This fruit. It's like the kind of antique Art people in high tiers have in their houses, except it's here for us all, outside."

Bristol immediately brightened, his chest swelling. "That's right!"

"That's what I thought when I first saw it this morning. I don't know if it's *right*, but that's my idea."

"No, I think you've really hit the nail on the—Samara, is that blood?"

Samara looked down to see a trail of red, darkened in the blue-tinted space, streaming down her leg. She froze. "I...yes, it is."

Bristol took out a handkerchief and handed it to her. She ran it up her leg to the hemline of her skirt.

"I didn't know Fives bleed too. I thought it was just unregistered," he said.

Samara looked up eagerly. "You bleed like this too? From the inside? Every day? Or does it stop and start?"

"No, I don't. It's just the women. I'm sorry. It happens for a few days every month. Is this...the first time?"

Samara nodded, told him about her lack of focus injections, and confessed she thought she'd be dead by this afternoon. She was glad when he did not laugh.

"You're not dying. Unregistered women cope just fine. They complain, but they live. If your stomach hurts, I could get you some pills."

Samara frowned. "I don't want any."

Bristol looked perplexed for a moment. He smiled and shook his head. "No, it's not what you think. Just medicine to help your stomach while it's happening. They don't have them in pharmacies."

"But you know where to get them?" Under her crossed arms, as if on cue, her insides contracted, and she winced.

"Let me bring them to you tonight. I'll just set them on the fire escape outside your window. If you want to take them, great—if not, just throw them out."

She looked at the handkerchief balled in her hand. "How will you get away? Aren't you chipped?"

He examined the bulge on the back of his hand. "You know, I'm not sure if this thing is even still active. It used to rumble sometimes when I was a kid, but it hasn't done that in years. It's ancient, though, and it only reads body heat. I just put a glove on, and then an ice pack under that, then I'm free."

"You can't be free. There are cameras everywhere."

"We've got ways around those too."

"It's a different life, being unregistered, isn't it?"

"Maybe. But we're not as different as you think."

"Why are you helping me?"

"I told you. I've got a vigilante nature." His eyes wandered over to the fruit. "And you're helping me too. I like talking about this."

"About art?"

"It's generous to call this art. But I do like hearing what you've got to say about it."

To her surprise, her dad wasn't drunk when she got home. Instead, he was drinking a glass of ice water and talking to her mom, whose face was projected on the white wall.

"Mom!"

"Baby!" said her mom's floating head. "How's my baby?"

Her dad's face was glowing, turning from mother to daughter.

"I'm fine," she stammered. She had just been wishing she could talk to her mom about her little problem, but now that she was here, Samara suddenly felt ashamed by it. She could just imagine what her mother would say: *What kind of a job doesn't provide focus injections?* The last thing her mom needed was more disappointment. "Fine! Things are going well. How are you?"

Her mom's image looked around, as if ensuring her privacy. "I'm fine, for now. But I was just telling your dad: I need to get out soon."

"I heard you were near a bad place."

"We are. And the worst part of it is that I think some of these people are involved. They're helping runaways."

"Where are they even running away to?"

"That's the craziest part. There aren't any more large cities to the north of us, so they're just fleeing to the country. North of us is just acres and acres of land and ruins of old cities. Unstable unregs are trying to just run up there and live off the land, I guess."

"Why don't you report it, Mom? Report the people around you if you think they're involved."

"If I do that and I'm wrong, I could be here picking berries for the rest of my life. And if someone reports me and I can't prove otherwise..."

Samara imagined her mother in prison, shoveling food down her throat to improve efficiency. She took her dad's hand. "We'll get you out. We're saving everything we can."

"I know you are. I love you, baby."

"I love you too."

After they said their goodbyes and ended the call, her dad wordlessly dumped the ice water down the sink and replaced it with bourbon, filling the glass to the top.

The next morning, there was a large red coffee mug on the fire escape with several carnation-pink pills inside. She rolled them around the bottom of the mug, wishing she knew for sure what Drift looked like. In the next room, her dad belched and groaned. With her hand still on the handle of the mug, she walked to the incinerator and tossed the pills in. Though it felt like she was being physically eaten from the inside, she couldn't afford the risk.

CHAPTER THIRTEEN

DENVER MARRIED STEPHEN ON A FRIDAY AFTERNOON, RIGHT after work. The whole thing had taken about four hours. Mrs. A. A. —a few weeks removed but barely recovered from her traumatic experience with the strange handyman no one seemed to know— arrived with Mr. Stephen Steiner already in tow and took them to another office to sign the necessary papers. After that, the three of them went to the cafeteria to eat a meal together. Denver had chosen a green salad with roasted peppers, almonds, tomatoes, and cucumbers. Normally she wouldn't have eaten anything so extravagant in front of a person of a lower tier, but this was her last time eating Three food. Fours ate cheaper ingredients because if everyone ate fresh fruits and vegetables, there wouldn't be enough to go around, obviously. They'd both received an adequate amount of information in each other's files. Mrs. A. A. was there to make suggestions of topics they might discuss. Mostly she just read the news on her watch, and when there was an awkward silence, she'd sigh and say things like, "Mmm...favorite sports teams? Ohh...what did you do last Saturday?" Whether Denver had anything interesting to say or not, she tried to keep talking to avoid another suggestion.

Every time A. A. cut in, Denver felt like the marriage was

getting off to a rocky start. She'd heard rumors that these officials could tell which marriages would last and which would end in divorce from the first meeting. The last thing she wanted to do was to imagine Mrs. A. A. going back to the water cooler, laughing about how sure she was that the mixed-tier couple would last the minimum sixteen years before splitting. Denver droned on, boring herself, until she caught Stephen's eyes flicker and his lips part to take in breath. While he talked, she thought of nothing but what to say next.

After dinner, they parted for the first and last time, each going back to their family homes for one more night.

"Can I see him?" asked Bristol.

Denver held out her wrist and projected his head in the air.

"He's...handsome!"

"I know." Denver's face was like stone, but she had a thought that brightened her. "By the way, I saw Allison today. She looks good. Might just be getting over you."

Bristol grinned. "I hope she and Mr. Ansberry can come through this together."

Denver laughed and shook her head. Then her face became more somber. "Can I ask you a favor?"

"You're reaching your limit."

"Hear me out," she said softly. "What you did at work...it was funny, but it's got to be the last time."

Bristol snorted. "I doubt they'd let me in again anyway."

"Shut up a second. I'm serious. It's a miracle you haven't been C-A-U-G-H-T yet." She glanced down at her watch. It remained still. "I'm going away and it'll just be you and Mom here. You need to stop now. Stop the painting and the practical jokes. Stop messing around with your life. If not for your own sake, then for Mom's."

"You're going to try and convince me that you care about Mom now? You two haven't spoken for weeks. Did you think I wouldn't notice? What's going on?"

"You're trying to change the subject. You promised you'd stop someday, and I'm asking you—no, I'm *telling* you—the time has to be now. That guy who was arrested for *your* painting is in prison right now. Don't do anything stupid."

"What are you afraid of? I'm always careful."

"Just—no more painting. No more revenge. And I know it's crossed your mind already—I *know* you, Bristol— do not turn yourself in."

Bristol lowered his shoulders and bowed his head slightly. "For the guy in prison. The innocent one?"

"Yes, him. I don't know what he was doing out after curfew either, but it couldn't have been good."

"Denver, *I'm* out after curfew almost every night!"

"Not anymore." Denver leaned in. "Promise."

Bristol looked at her and nodded. "Okay."

Denver left him and stepped inside the bathroom. Once inside and alone with her thoughts, she reached for her watch but felt only her bare wrist. She'd taken it off at the door. She was technically married now. This had been what she was waiting on to be happy. Her last night with Bristol and Mom, and all she could do was pick fights and lock herself away. She pressed her fingertips into her temples. *Get it together.*

She undressed and ran water in the tub. For once, she didn't care if she exceeded her water allowance for the month—that was a problem for another day. In the mirror, she played with different angles to guess at her best side. She looked toned from straight-on, though a little flabby from the side. She sucked in her gut and looked again. Better. Something bizarre caught her eye—was one of her breasts bigger than the other? Why hadn't she noticed before? She felt with her hands, confirming the imbalance. This threw off the look of straight-on. She closed her eyes, blew a long breath out, and made a mental note to make sure to be seen from the left.

Denver liked her bath scalding, even in June. It made her sweat, but she didn't care because it seemed she could finally feel all the little muscles in her legs and feet relax. She had a friend once who said she had a hard time "letting go." A boy named Harold. She'd met him in the eighth grade and used to fantasize from time to time about being paired with him. But that had stopped suddenly one day a few years later when he told her she was trying too hard for her future.

"I mean, why do you even study for these things?" he asked her after she had, once again, beaten him for the top grade in a test. "It's not like you're going to stay a Three. You have a brother."

"I'm going to get a Three job," she said.

"I know, but then they'll pair you. And then you'll just be a Four." He waved his hand over the projection of the posted scores on the classroom wall. "This doesn't really matter for you. Just let it go."

Denver still felt the sting. And all these years later, he was right, of course. She tilted her head up to stop the tears in her eyes from falling into the bathwater. *Just let it go.*

The next day was moving day. Bristol and their mother helped carry in a few boxes of Denver's things and arrange furniture in the new apartment across town, a glistening copper building that smelled like paint. New units were still being constructed, so the sounds of construction could be heard, which came in handy, as Stephen's parents were also helping and there were plenty of awkward pauses to fill. It was, at least, much better than the marriage official demanding never-ending conversation.

Behind the door marked 801, after the sofa was in its final location and the families had left, the newlyweds tried eying each other without being caught. Finally, Stephen spoke.

"I'm hungry."

"Me too." Denver had just realized it. "Neither of us has eaten since breakfast."

"I'd like some rice and beans," her new husband said.

"That sounds good."

The two of them looked at each other. In a beat, Denver understood.

"Oh." She stood as he sat on the sofa along the right side of the wall. "Oh."

In the kitchen, she fumbled, opening several cabinet doors before remembering where they'd put the pans. It wasn't until she filled it with water that she became indignant. What was a Four doing in there lounging while she made his dinner? She couldn't set this expectation. She let the water boil. Then she walked back into the family room.

"You know, I could use some help. In my house, my mother cooked."

Her first lie.

"Oh," Stephen said. "My mother did too. I don't think I can be of much help." Blood rushed to his light cheeks.

"That's okay. It might be fun to figure it out together."

His smile was quick. He rose from the sofa and followed her into the kitchen, where the first little bubbles had begun to appear in the water on the stove.

Stephen peered into the pot. "Good, you've got the water going. What should we put in there, the beans or the rice? Or both?"

Now Denver smiled. "Let's go with the rice."

She let Stephen pour nearly the entire package of rice into the water, but she heated the can of beans herself. Stephen retrieved two plates from the cupboard. He looked at the stove.

"So...we wait?"

She shrugged. She would not allow his incompetence to define her role in this house. What if there were other things he couldn't do? She couldn't possibly do all the work expected of her at the office and cook every meal for him as well.

"Maybe you should check and see if it's hot enough yet."

He took a single grain of rice out of the warm water and tasted it. "No, it's hard."

"I think it'll get softer if we leave it in there for longer."

"We can try that," he said. "So your mom did all the cooking too? What about your dad? Where was he today?"

"My dad is...deceased. A train ran him over when I was young."

"Gosh, I'm so sorry. Why was he so close to the tracks? Was he an engineer?"

She winced. "No. No, we think he...wanted to go."

Stephen appeared to be at a loss for words. Finally, he said, "So... your mom handles everything alone?"

"Yes, but my brother cooks too. He works in a kitchen." She looked up. "Have you ever met an unreg before today?"

Stephen's eyes did a funny twitch. "Have I? An unreg? Yes, I think so. Some of them clean our building at night, so when I work late I say hi sometimes."

Denver snorted. "You two sort of sound alike, you and Bristol."

"How do you mean?"

But then Denver realized what she'd meant. That was the voice Bristol used when trying to convince Mom that he'd been asleep in his bed all night, trying to hide the paint still under his fingernails. "Nothing. Never mind."

Stephen looked over her shoulder. "Denver? Is the rice supposed to be getting bigger?"

There was a small mountain of rice rising out of the pot, so they quickly transferred it into a bigger one. Soon, they were straining the small can of beans and weeks' worth of rice and carrying their plates to the little table built for three. Denver picked up her fork, but Stephen put a hand on hers.

"Denver? Could I ask you something?"

She put her fork down and drew her hand away. "Sure."

"In my family, we do this thing before we eat anything. You just say something you're thankful for."

"Before you eat *anything*?"

"Well, any meal."

"Every meal? Every day?"

"Yes. What do you think?"

She thought it was the stupidest thing she'd ever heard of. But as she'd just spent the first evening of their marital life lying to him, she thought it better not to say this.

"Okay."

Stephen lowered his chin as if he were about to face-plant into his food, but stopped, thankfully, so his forehead hovered above the table. He closed his eyes. "I am thankful for this dinner, our new home, and for my wife."

That last word sent an electric current through Denver's skin. Stephen looked up at her before she was ready.

"Now you," he said.

"I...I am thankful for those things too." The words were clunky and ran into an uncomfortable pause when she was deciding whether or not to also give thanks for her husband. But the pause ended, and Stephen picked up his fork and began to eat. *Just as well,* thought Denver. They were only married on paper. They weren't real lovers. Just two strangers, not to be trusted with the others' secrets.

CHAPTER FOURTEEN

COMPARED TO THE OTHER BOYS IN SAMARA'S CLASSES, JUDE STOOD out as charmingly naive—the way he talked about being free perplexed her and everyone else he mentioned it to. He obviously believed there'd been some sort of a mix-up that led to his arrest, but Samara didn't have the heart to tell him that you didn't just *get out* of prison. It took years of appeals and unbreakable DNA-based evidence of innocence. Metrics was all about strength and superiority, or at least the appearance of it, and the strong and superior would be less so if they allowed their cracks to be seen. But Jude seemed like the type of person who believed he could make things happen out of sheer will, as if the unthinkable could be reversed if only due to his own resolve, and Samara liked him for that.

He had taken up the habit of cornering her in the yard when she had outdoor duty and peppering her with questions. She didn't mind, but his questions did finally give her some insight as to what the warden was talking about. One day, for example, he asked her:

"How do you know if you're making a good choice?"

"What do you mean?" she'd asked.

"I mean"—he scrunched his sweaty nose to keep his glasses from sliding down any further—"when you have a choice to make, is there any real way to know it's the right choice? Sometimes when I'm making the license plates, I can see a little imperfection, but if I stop to fix it, it might take me longer than the thirty-six seconds. We're only supposed to have each one in our hands for thirty-six seconds. So what's more important? Quality or time?"

Remembering what the warden had said about his mental disorder around this issue, she reminded him that the right way was always the way he'd been taught. "If the time limit is thirty-six seconds, then that's all the time you get. If the shop manager notices any major differences in quality, then they'll adjust. But think of it this way: what if every boy took longer to make the plates?"

Jude scratched at his temple. "It'd affect efficiency."

"Exactly. Smart boy. Also, everyone may have a different standard of quality. You may have it on your station for two minutes, then the next boy in line may have it for ten seconds. There'd be no way to measure how many plates to expect to get done in a day!"

Jude was quiet, and Samara had congratulated herself on getting through to him. Maybe she could convince the warden he wasn't a danger after all.

"Unless," Jude said, interrupting her internal back-pat, "they waited for a month and took the average."

"Okay, Jude, almost time for the bell. Move it."

But today, Jude asked no questions. He sat alone in the yard, not speaking to anyone. It was odd, but then with Jude, odd was what she'd come to expect. It wasn't until she realized Kopecky was also sulking that she decided to get involved.

"What's wrong, Albin?" she asked him, and he bowed his head so low that the wrinkles in his thick neck disappeared.

"Nothing."

"You can tell me. Are you having an argument with your friend? Do you remember your script for this situation?"

"I'm not talking to him with no script."

"Exactly, scripts are very useful for this kind of thing. Just say—"

"No, Miss Shepherd. I'm worried about him."

Still taken aback at his interruption, Samara huffed. Why didn't these boys seem as afraid of her as they were of the guards? But Kopecky didn't even seem to understand what he'd done; he just looked down at his hands, opening and closing them. "See, Miss Shepherd—I think someone here's got something against him. Maybe a guard. In our cell this morning—"

Samara's watch flashed blue.

"That's ridiculous," said Samara. "If you need help with the friendship reconciliation script, I can help you practice. Otherwise, I want no more nonsense."

"Yes, ma'am," said Kopecky, eyeing the flashing light on her wrist.

Samara went home after work with two questions on her mind. What had happened in Jude's cell this morning, and was he in danger? The answer to the first was relatively easy to discover. All she had to do was request access to security videos, which she tried in her bedroom. She was surprised to find she had full access. She watched security videos for an hour before she looked up Jude's cell, as not to draw attention to what she was searching for. Finally, she typed in the location and the evening before the surprise inspection. The evening before, one of the guards had clearly gone in, slipped something under his mattress, and walked away. The cameras were turned off at night and activated by ancient motion detectors, so because Jude had stayed close to his bed when he'd gotten up the next morning, she wasn't able to see anything more until the morning inspection. The warden had gone completely mad looking for whatever the guard had placed under his mattress. Samara was impressed with Jude; watching the video again, it was doubtless he'd found the drugs and hidden them under his foot—it was all in the way he was standing, which she wouldn't have noticed if she hadn't had close contact with him every day.

To discover whether or not Jude was in real danger was trickier. There was no need, the warden had told her, to have contact with any staff at the detention center. The guards rarely spoke except for one-word commands, and the kitchen staff had never said a word. She suspected they'd also been warned that they were not to have contact with anyone else either. People grumble and commiserate when they're allowed to talk to one another at work. Warden Paul seemed to know this and had the good sense to nip it in the bud. After seeing what the guard had done, Samara thought it would be safer to ask the kitchen staff.

The next day, when the unregistered woman set out Samara's bowl of gray oatmeal on the countertop, Samara said, "Thank you." The woman smiled.

The day after that, she looked down at the plate of drying rice and shriveled broccoli and said, "Thanks. Looks delicious." The woman smirked, which worried her at first, but then the two caught eyes and Samara could see the woman assumed she'd been joking.

Samara sensed she was running out of time to be coy, so she waited until her class was over and approached the woman again, who was on her hands and knees scrubbing a corner of the kitchen. She saw no need to beat around the bush—if someone saw her, they'd both be in trouble, so it was better to get it over with quickly.

"The boys who are sent away from here," Samara said. "Where do they go?"

At first she wasn't sure the woman had heard her. She just continued scrubbing, the little joints in her fingers bright red with effort. Samara considered walking away, but the woman spoke. "Bad place."

"A work camp? The country?" asked Samara.

"No," said the woman, and Samara leaned in to hear her whisper above the hiss of the scrub brush on the tile. "A lab. Without lab rats."

After a moment, Samara understood. "Why do they go there?"

"The warden sends them."

"If they do something wrong first," Samara corrected her. "What kinds of offenses can get them sent away?"

The woman stopped cleaning, stood, and squared herself to Samara. "The warden sends them."

CHAPTER FIFTEEN

JUDE WASN'T PREPARED FOR THIS. HE COULDN'T REMEMBER THE last time he didn't know exactly what to do. In school, there was a protocol for every type of problem imaginable. Students were well practiced in hundreds of individual problem-solving techniques. For lost homework, you ask the teacher to search your watch with her find device. If a dog bit you in the street, just bring your whistle to your lips and blow five short blasts and one long one. If you had a friend who liked sniffing glue a little too much, you take the glue, give it to the teacher, and simply say your friend's name. They never taught you what to do if you were the sniffer. Wait for a friend to solve your problem for you, he guessed.

There was a right way through every situation. Even when he was arrested, he'd remained calm and remembered that's what you do when you're wrongfully accused: steady yourself and wait for the truth to come out. But the truth hadn't, not yet, and he was beginning to fear that Kopecky had been right all along. He'd been set up, probably by the school because he was an outlier ruining their stats and throwing off their averages. The best he could hope for now was that his mother missed him and hadn't gotten pregnant yet with his replacement. Maybe if she and his father started asking some questions, they could get him out...

But Jude would have to get rid of this bag first.

The raid yesterday morning seemed far away. Surely the warden knew by now where he'd hidden the bag, but somehow he still had it in his pocket throughout his lesson with Miss Shepherd.

In their lessons, they were relearning how to spell and sound out words. It seemed a little ridiculous, since he'd learned to do this when he was four. But several inmates who had been here for about that long—Kopecky included—hadn't mastered it yet and seemed actively determined not to start now. As if to apologize for his classmates, Jude had participated in lessons more than ever, but it had set a bad precedent: now that he was counting on an hour of quiet to work out what to do with this bag, Miss Shepherd wouldn't leave him alone. He answered the questions about vowel sounds absentmindedly at first, then irritably. When the first bell rang, he stayed in his seat. It was just a warning bell, and they still had a few minutes before they cleared the room, but they could tell Miss Shepherd was finished teaching for the day. Jude was still, trying to take advantage of every second he was still allowed to be there.

"What's wrong, Jude?" said Miss Shepherd beside him.

He cringed. Was a few seconds of silence too much to ask for? "Nothing, miss."

He got up to join the single-file line forming near the door, but his papers dropped and splattered off onto the floor. Kopecky crouched down to help. "We've got it, Miss Shepherd," he said to her as she made a motion to do the same.

"Jeeze, kid," Kopecky said when she'd walked away. "All these little words...what are you doing here?"

He was referring to Jude's notebooks, where he wrote letters to no one in the margins when he couldn't take the monotony of phonics lessons anymore.

"Those are just...I just write when I get bored. Don't want to waste paper, so it's better to write small."

"Didja write anything today?" asked Kopecky, looking over his shoulder.

"I wasn't bored today."

"That makes one of us."

Kopecky handed him his notebook.

"You're talking to me again," Jude said.

"Yeah. I've been thinking, and I think you're probably smart not to tell anybody what you did. God knows I could stay outta some trouble if I just learned to shut my mouth every now and then. But if you do wanna tell somebody, you can tell me."

Jude did. He told him about the drugs and quickly recounted the story of how they ended up in his pocket.

Kopecky's eyes widened. "I knew it. They've got it out for you. Why would they put you in prison and then try to frame you again in here?" He swallowed and looked away. "Unless..."

"What?"

"Well, there's this other place—it's a prison too, I guess—where they send the kids who are too bad for this place. Kids who do stuff like that." He nodded to Jude's pocket. "Looks like sending you here wasn't enough. Whoever wants you gone really doesn't want you to come back."

"You don't come back from...the other place?"

"No. I've heard things...like there, you don't do work, you *are* the work. They do experiments on you and stuff."

Jude shuddered.

"You can't go there," Kopecky said. "So what are we going to do?"

Taken aback at the we, Jude gaped at him. But there was no time for processing; the second bell was about to ring. "I don't know. I feel like I should ask for help, but who'd help me?"

Kopecky seemed to also sense the urgency and spoke faster. "Someone who likes you. Someone who can get outside. Someone who has power, but not too much of it."

"Boys, I think you're done there." Miss Shepherd's feet had appeared beside him. "Join the line, please."

Kopecky whipped his head around and grinned widely at Jude. "Yes, ma'am. By the way, my friend needs to talk to you."

"Of course," said Miss Shepherd. The inmates left the room, several glancing back to see if Jude would join them. Jude made some parting motions as though he was about to leave, but hung back right at the door. Miss Shepherd took his shoulder and led him into the hall.

"Whatever it is," said Miss Shepherd in a low tone, hardly moving her lips, "you'll have to give it to me out in the yard."

"The yard?"

"You'll understand in..." She looked down at her watch. "Twenty seconds. Let's move, join your classmates."

Jude hadn't gone three steps before the fire alarm went off.

Minutes later, all the inmates were in the yard. As Jude was the last person in line, Miss Shepherd had tasked him with carrying her books. The warden and the guards patrolled the lines of boys who stood obediently with their palms pressed into the sides of their hips.

"How did you do that?" whispered Jude.

"Do what?" Miss Shepherd asked.

Jude remembered what Kopecky had said about avoiding trouble by keeping quiet and decided didn't need to know, anyway. He kept his eyes forward and lowered his right hand into his pocket, produced the bag and swiftly hid it on the inside cover of the top book. One of the guards must have seen the cover move, because she came over and said, "All boys must stand at attention during fire drills, Miss Shepherd."

"Sorry," said Miss Shepherd and took the books from Jude, pressing them to her chest.

"No problem," the guard said. "I heard this was your idea, Miss Shepherd."

"They do surprise fire drills at the higher-tier schools nowadays. I simply suggested it to the warden. I'm glad she approved it."

Jude pressed his hand on his trousers, took in the outside of his empty pocket with his fingertips, and felt delirious with a strange sensation—for the first time, someone had risked something for him for no reason; he hadn't had to earn this kindness or prove he was worthy of it, it was just given. For the first time in eleven years, Jude had been shown love.

CHAPTER SIXTEEN

BRISTOL WASHED AND DRIED HIS HANDS AGAIN AND THEN LOOKED up at the little white screen for the next order. He reached into the oven for the potato, opened it, and stacked the ingredients. Reciting the little list in his head helped his hands to work fast: *cheesesourcreambutterchives.* The abundance of dairy on this order made him certain this was for a Three. His sister was forever gobbling yogurt, especially in the weeks leading up to her marriage and demotion, when she'd no longer be able to buy it.

The kitchen manager, who looked perpetually on the edge of breaking the silence with fanatical screaming, marched over to his station, pointed at the potato, and said, "Now!"

Bristol threw it on a plate and tossed it to him, savoring the momentum of his movements.

The kitchen staff wore all black, so it was striking when the owner walked by in his blue button-down shirt and yellow-striped tie. Whatever his name was, he usually only stayed a few minutes to tell the kitchen manager that table eleven was in a hurry or someone had messed up and put beans on a plate when they should have given it bread. But this time, he walked right past the kitchen manager, and Bristol had only a moment to brace himself as he realized the owner was headed in his direction.

He got closer to Bristol and looked at him in the eye. "You make the soup?" he asked.

Bristol nodded, and the man smiled and said, "You have an admirer. Says it's so good that she wants to thank you."

Bristol froze. Was this a trick? He'd never heard anything of the kind in his six years of working here.

The owner squeezed his shoulder. "I'm saying I want you to come with me. Hang your apron there and walk out into the dining room so she can say thanks. I can show you where she's sitting."

He took off his apron and followed him. They rounded the corner, and his eyes and ears worked to adjust from the bright, stark light and clanging in the kitchen to the soft, dim dining room, where the same quiet jazz song played all day, so low you wouldn't notice it if you weren't listening. After a few steps, he saw a familiar face in the distance, framed by cinnamon curls. He quickly looked down and tried to brush some flour from his sleeve. They stopped at her table, where she was eating alone.

"Miss, here's the cook that prepared your soup tonight," said the man in the yellow tie.

Samara looked up at Bristol with a strange look. Was it relief? She looked at him like he'd just rescued her kitten from a tree. "Oh, thank you! Yes, the soup was excellent."

"We don't get many requests like this," the owner told her. "But then again, we don't get many Fives in here, either! Mostly we're a low Three, high Four establishment. They're all used to this caliber of cuisine, I think, so they don't make a fuss. It's nice to hear some gratitude!"

Bristol felt his face redden. What was she doing here, and what was this meal costing her? "Thank you," he said. "It's really a simple recipe."

"Quality ingredients make the difference!"

The owner wasn't unkind, and never passed on an opportunity to have his ego stroked, so it didn't surprise Bristol that he'd obliged and brought him into the dining room. But the lights in here were too low and Samara was a little too beautiful in them, and he felt the intense desire to walk out the door, preferably with her.

"Yes," said Samara, holding out a small white plate, and on it, a butter knife and with something wrapped in a napkin. "The only thing is...well, the bread that came with it...I hate to say...had a piece of mold on it."

The owner looked thunderstruck. Bristol locked eyes with Samara and, as if rehearsed, grabbed the plate from her.

"Don't unwrap it. I wouldn't want to cause a scene. Would you just throw it in the incinerator, there?" She pointed directly behind Bristol, and before the owner could object, Bristol took the napkin from the plate and threw it into the incinerator. He'd been putting those dinner rolls on plates and scraping them off again for years. Whatever was wrapped inside was no dinner roll. In his right hand, he nervously twirled the butter knife. Samara gave him a strange look, but he was sure he'd imagined it a second later because she just smiled and thanked the owner again.

Bristol and his boss walked back into the kitchen, where Bristol expected to be berated in front of his coworkers. Tossing napkins in the incinerator was strictly against the rules, and he'd never broken a rule at work before, nor had anyone else. But if he'd had any objections to Bristol's behavior or thought that encounter was strange, he made no indication. He squeezed Bristol's shoulder again, congratulated him, and left.

At the end of his shift, Bristol pulled on his orange vest, indicating he was allowed to be out past curfew, and walked home, thinking of the paint combinations he could play with to recreate her eye color. Sort of a brown-red, but he'd like to see them again in the light. And then in the darkness too. He walked a block and a half past his front door. He realized it and laughed quietly. Now he knew why Denver and all the other registered kids received those focus injections every week from the time they were twelve—the opposite sex could be distracting. How would he see her if he was registered? She'd be just another person, as surely he was to her, no different from her bus driver or Yellow-tie Man or even her future spouse. The thought made his fists ball up and his stomach rise.

He opened the door to another surprise: Denver shrieked at the sight of him and pulled him into a back-breaking hug.

"What are you doing here?" he asked as loudly as his compressed lungs would allow.

"Stephen's working late, so I got special permission to spend the night here! How have you been?"

Unable to hold it in, he told her all about Samara at the restaurant. As he was talking, he realized how much he'd missed his sister in the few weeks she'd been away. No one listened like she did, quietly engaged until he was really finished.

"Are you going to turn her in?" she asked.

"What? No! She's my..."

"Friend?"

"Well, kind of. I think she wants to be my friend anyway. Or I want to be hers."

"Friendship is built on trust. What reason has she given you to trust her?"

Bristol quietly considered.

"She's very pretty."

Denver scoffed and rolled her eyes. She started to say something, but Bristol wasn't listening. Something was dawning on him. The look Samara had given him when he spun her knife. Did she know? Were they friends?

Denver sighed and continued. "Trust but verify. It's an ancient piece of advice, but it's good. At Domestic Affairs, we watch, we listen, we follow... Pretty much every aspect of a person's life is trackable nowadays. A lot of the time, they give much more information than what we ask for. All you have to do is get her ID number and her life will be so open you'll feel like she's your other sister."

They had never had this conversation before. Bristol had never felt entitled to ask. "What kind of information do you get at DA?"

"Oh, lots of stuff. We can use the GPS to see everywhere she goes. Use the meal tracker to know what she eats and how much. We can see the other IDs around her to know who she's talking with. We can even see what time she goes to sleep and wakes up based on her blood pressure and breathing patterns. It's all in the watch, and then it's all on our wall." Denver tapped her watch to project a bright white rectangle on the wall in front of the sofa. "ID search," she said clearly into the face. The white rectangle displayed her words and added, *Please type the ID number.*

Denver looked to Bristol. "Well? Do you know it?"

He did. He had seen the number on her watchband the first day he met her, which had been emblazoned into his mind ever since. The temptation to know what she was doing at this moment was too great. He heard himself saying them.

"Five-two-four-nine-two-seven."

Immediately, her picture appeared.

"Now this is what everyone can see—"

Bristol snickered. "Everyone with a watch."

"Yes, everyone with a watch, if they know her number. So here you can see her favorite foods, her family tree, her games and her high scores...not much of a game player..."

Bristol searched the screen, greedily trying to pick up as much of Samara as possible. She liked baked carrots and blackberries. She had a mother and a father who looked kind. She hadn't played any games in the past year.

"Interesting," said Denver suddenly.

"What is?"

"She's a *Five*, but she's an education manager!"

"Yeah, at a juvenile detention center."

"Yes, but still, that's impressive." She smiled. "She must be smart."

"I think she is. What's she doing right now?"

"I need to enter my access code to see..." Bristol mouthed the numbers with her. "Three-three-seven-two-two-two. Here we go. She's home. That's good. It's saying that both the soup and the bread registered for her dinner."

"Will she get in trouble?"

"Did your boss seem to think she was up to no good?"

"I don't think so."

"Then, no, if you don't report it." Denver's hand hovered over her watch. "But I think you should. Do you want to report it?"

"No! I mean, she must have had a reason. Denver, you can't tell anyone about this, okay?"

"I won't. But you should probably cut ties with this girl. I don't know what she did to land that education job, but people in her tier would do almost anything for a position like that. She might have something up her sleeve that you don't want to get pulled into."

"Like what?"

"Some people can manipulate the system—for a little while. But they always get caught eventually. They'll break into official records and screw things up. Sometimes we get Fives who write different diet logs to make it look like they're eating all their food, for example, but they're not. Then they lose weight and tell us they need more food vouchers, more calories. When actually they're trying to feed...someone."

"Someone like me?"

"Yes, frankly."

"I thought you and mom got extra vouchers for me."

Denver fell silent.

"Denver, how do my vouchers get here?"

"You can also get extra vouchers...if you work for them."

"What do you mean?"

"Mom and I work a few extra hours a week each to get an extra booklet for you. I thought you knew."

Bristol's stomach was heavy. "I didn't."

"It's not a big deal."

There was a long silence, and then Bristol looked up. "How many?"

"Not many."

"How many?"

Denver sighed. "Bristol, it's a small sacrifice for a big reward." Her voice broke. "I love having a brother."

"They don't feed us. What do they expect us to do?" He looked at his sister. "Tell me the truth. Do they want us to die?"

Denver licked her lips and drew a breath in. "No." She lowered her shoulders and lifted her head. "No, of course not. They know the wanted unregs are well cared for. That's what family is for."

"And the unwanted?"

"No one is unwanted. Everyone comes from a family."

Now their mother's voice could be heard from the thin wall behind the still-glowing projected screen. "Some people in the family gotta work early in the morning!"

Denver was in her old bed and asleep in minutes, a skill that had always made Bristol jealous. He closed his eyes, vaguely aware of the scent of rosemary seeped deep into his skin. When he couldn't resist anymore, he sat up, threw the blanket at his feet, and rummaged under the bed for his sketchpad. The light given by the window was all he needed for a couple of simple sketches. He moved quickly for a few minutes, then had a realization that slowed the drag of his pencil until it came to a complete stop. She was the instructor at Fox County Detention Center. That's where he was—the kid. They knew each other, they had to. He got up and paced around the house. It's true that it wasn't fair. The kid hadn't painted that nun. Maybe he deserved to be in prison, hidden away from paints and bricks and his family and...

He swallowed. *No.* No, he couldn't do it. He'd made his promise to Denver, and it was true that he was all Mom had. He'd try to stay away from Samara—right after he made sure she was okay.

He tossed his notebook on the floor, where it caught a ray of light from the window. There were two sketches—a carrot, a blackberry.

CHAPTER SEVENTEEN

AFTER THE RESTAURANT, SAMARA CAME HOME AND UNLOCKED HER window. She had a feeling she hadn't seen the last of Bristol tonight. Not that she knew anything about him, not personally, but if his murals were any indication of his character, he wasn't the type to do something without questioning it. She was almost sure he'd turn up to ask her what was in the napkin, and possibly ask a favor in return. Favors, her father was fond of saying, were a valuable currency. You could give them to anyone, but you had to be careful who you accepted them from, because they'd always come back around. She already owed him for the pills to calm her stomach, even though she hadn't taken them, but asking him to dispose of drugs in front of his boss had been much costlier. She was exhausted from helping Jude, but she wouldn't forget this kindness of Bristol's.

Just before midnight, she heard the little chime of a pebble hitting the side of the iron fire escape. She grinned, stuck her hand out, and gestured for him to come up.

The fire escape was too small for Bristol's stocky build, and he looked awkward squeezed between the iron bars and her window. She sat on the ledge anyway and didn't back away from the window, though it was almost necessary. He contorted his limbs until he found a shape that suited him.

"Hi," she said.

"Hi."

"Aren't you going to ask me what I was doing at your restaurant today?"

"Aren't you going to invite me in?"

Samara pursed her lips. Metrics catching an unreg in her window was one thing. Her father catching him was another.

"Please," he said with strain in his voice, "this thing is pinching my legs."

Her father snored in the next room. She stood back and let Bristol untangle onto her floor. He cracked the joints in his neck.

"Better?"

"Somewhat." He looked around her room, and Samara began to see her own room through his eyes. When she did, she noticed her shoes carelessly thrown on the floor, the damp clothes drying on the rack. But Bristol didn't seem interested in her messes—he crossed her room and hummed lowly, kneeling beside her old wooden rocking horse.

"What's this?" he asked and reached out his hands to touch it. He put two gentle hands on the horse's head and tail, studying it.

"My great-grandfather made that. It's a toy."

"Toys are illegal. Physical toys, anyway. Adults are still allowed their toys." Bristol gestured toward Samara's watch.

"No, physical toys are illegal unless they're educational. My parents made the argument that this one is. See, you sit on it, and told on to these handles, and rock yourself. Wanna try?"

"If I wanted another cramp in my legs, I'd go back out on the fire escape."

"It's easier when you're little."

"Wait, how is this educational?"

"Well, when you rock, it can be rhythmic, so my parents recorded me on it reciting different things: the Pledge of Allegiance, the

Metrics values. See?" She rocked it with her hand, emphasizing the words as the horse's head dipped toward the floor. "'I pledge allegiance to the crest of the Metrics worldwide government. And to the idea that we create an ideal people with gifts for obedience, resilience, and silence through careful measurement of our potential'—and so on, you know the rest. They claimed it was easier for me to memorize information because it was linked to activity, and it helped that I was the first in my class to memorize these things."

"I'll bet they expected you to keep being the first."

"That was the condition on which they agreed to let us keep it, yes. And after a few years, they stopped asking Mom and Dad to prove it was still working. They haven't asked about it in a long time. And I guess it worked—I'm good at regurgitating information."

"The Metrics dream girl."

Samara frowned. From anyone else, that would be a compliment, but Bristol's tone was undeniably mocking.

"Tonight should have been your first clue that I'm anything but a model citizen. Isn't that what you came here for? To ask me what happened?"

"I'm no model citizen either."

Samara resisted the urge to point out he wasn't a citizen at all. Instead, she just twisted her features and cocked her head as if to say, *Meaning?*

"Meaning that I've handled enough Drift in my day to know what a massive bag of it feels like, even wrapped in a napkin."

"Well," said Samara, growing impatient, "Don't you want to know what I was doing with it?"

"Not really."

"Then why are you here? To collect your return favor?"

Bristol's expression changed into one of surprise and hurt. "Not at all. I won't claim I'm not curious—I am—but I'm here because I'm worried about you. Drift can seem like it'll solve all your problems, Samara, but after the effects wear off, you're just back at your life again, with the same problems and a few more."

It took a few moments for Samara to understand, but when she did, her brow released from its scrunch. "You thought I was using! No, you misunderstood." She told him about Jude and the warden.

Bristol actually giggled, despite the seriousness of the situation. "You may be the first to smuggle drugs *out* of a prison."

"And hopefully the last."

"Well, what if the warden plants them on him again? He's going to come to you again for help. What are you going to do?"

Samara hadn't thought of that. Truthfully, she wished she hadn't gotten involved at all, but she felt she had no other choice. She couldn't let an innocent little boy be carted away to a place more hellish than the one he was already in.

"Why did you even do it at all?"

"Because he didn't deserve it," said Samara. "He doesn't even deserve to be there. He was arrested for that." She nodded out the window to the wall that had once displayed Bristol's nun, now whitewashed into nothing. Bristol's eyes gave him away; he knew what had been there before. He knew Jude wasn't to blame. "He's just a low-performing Two, and there aren't supposed to be low-performing Twos. Instead of just letting him live his life, Metrics is trying to erase him and claim their genetic experiment is flawless."

Bristol turned back to the rocking horse, tracing a finger over the brown, pointed ears. "It makes me angry too. I don't blame you for wanting to help."

"I appreciate you coming over and giving me the chance to explain myself. I won't trouble you again."

"I hope you do. If it happens again, just give me a signal. Do you still have the coffee cup I put those pills in?" Samara nodded. "Just put that out on your fire escape. I'll come by and look, and if I see it—"

Samara raised her eyebrows. "You're going to come by every night, just to check?"

Bristol didn't skip a beat. "Yes."

"That seems safe," Samara scoffed.

"Safe for your student. He's counting on you now. And like it or not, you're counting on me." Bristol drew himself up to his full height, taking up space in her little room. He looked much bigger in here than he did in the restaurant, next to the man in the ridiculous tie.

"Why do you want to be involved?"

"It's the least I can do."

She knew exactly what he meant, but she wanted to hear him say it: *because I'm the real artist.* "What's that supposed to mean?"

He hesitated, then reached out and pushed on the horse's tail, rocking it a few times. "I've been in trouble before, and there were always people around to help me. I'm just paying it forward." Samara noted how he avoided her eyes. "Guess you've got to get up early for work?"

"I do. But I'm glad you came, Bristol, I really am. Thank you."

Bristol turned down her blanket and fluffed her pillow. Samara watched him, shocked at the intimacy of the gesture. Something about it was so familiar, so domestic; it was the first time anyone had readied her bed for her, but she felt it could have been the hundredth time. Without letting herself overthink it, she walked over and sat in her bed. Bristol lifted her legs in and covered them with her blanket. He looked at her with his deep brown eyes and smiled, and she returned it. She had a strange urge to ask him to stay until she fell asleep, but she'd already asked way too much of him today, and it was a bizarre thing to ask anyone to do.

"Good night," he said, and though the words usually meant parting, he didn't move.

"Good night."

His hand was so close to hers. "I'll watch for that cup."

"Take care of yourself, Bristol."

"You too."

He climbed out the window.

Samara eased herself down into her puffy pillow, knowing this strange thrill she felt wouldn't allow her to sleep anytime soon. That he was unregistered, and that she had no reason to hope for a future together wouldn't matter at all, at least not tonight. He was her artist, he was sincere, and he wanted to help. Her heart hummed. For tonight, it was enough.

CHAPTER EIGHTEEN

Denver's marriage wasn't going well. No, it *was* going well, but that was the problem. She was well acquainted with mediocrity, having grown up as a Three, but she'd never quite accepted her lot. When she was ten she was ruined for mediocrity forever, the day she'd become fascinated with an idea long forgotten, in the public library. It was an idea back from a time when there were separate countries, imaginary lines drawn to separate one place from another, and every place had something special about it. In America, it had been the simple idea that people could, through hard work, change their station in life. Even the name of this idea had a stirring, hopeful ring to it: the American Dream.

Such a silly thing, such a thinly veiled tactic to increase productivity, as she well knew from her time at the DA, and yet even in her adulthood, Denver couldn't let it go. Work hard and change your life. She badly wanted to believe that, somehow, an energy in the world existed that would allow this to happen, and so she began trying harder, and sometimes it would work for her, sometimes not. Threes were all exempt from manual labor, and most of them worked in offices, double-checking that technology was doing its job and reporting or repairing when it did not.

Denver found she had a knack for anticipating problems in the systems and genuinely liked doing anything that wasn't really her job. Talking with people, programming the system to be more efficient, noticing which households could improve their energy use by doing something simple, sending letters to let them know. Sometimes she'd see their rations go up because of her suggestions. All she really *had* to do was sit there and make sure the computer's monitoring seemed right and get up to bring coffee and sandwiches to her boss, but something about that task made her feel like a computer herself. Anyone off the street could do that.

And she was beginning to think anyone off the street could also be married to Stephen.

He would arrive home a little earlier than she did, and he would immediately begin playing games on the sofa. He didn't even have the common courtesy to project a screen so she could watch. He just sat staring at the tiny screen, huffing every now and then, as if he were doing real work. When she came in, he'd say hello and go back to his games. She held out on making dinner for him for as long as she could, but eventually she grew tired of his daily "What's for dinner?" and he seemed to suspect she knew more about cooking than she was letting on. He'd take his plate back to the sofa to play more games and then leave it there for her to pick up. The little melodies and rings and dings coming from the watch drove her mad. She'd begun waking up earlier than she would have liked because he'd keep the door to the bathroom closed while he got ready all morning long, and she didn't want to go in there with him to witness what he could be doing.

They did not fight, but they didn't talk either. For his part, Stephen did not seem to notice the physical toll it had taken on Denver to work so hard after work, nor did he notice her lack of interest in their mandatory weekly lovemaking sessions on Sunday afternoons. Before he could even roll over to his own side, she'd click the Completed box next to the flashing red reminder, relieved to see it stop. Once, he'd attempted to stroke her cheek after it was over.

She laid perfectly still and let him do it, let him sense her chill. That, at least, satisfied her in a way.

On Sundays, they were excused from an additional hour of work to attend an Introduction to Marriage class. Everyone was the same age, but Denver had to go to the Fours class, where everyone showed up in their dirty clothes, smelling of oil or cleaning fluid or sweat. One other girl, Maureen, had also married down a tier and relentlessly tempted Denver with co-misery and gossip about the other girls. Denver did her best to avoid her and ignore her spiteful asides, though too often Maureen said what she herself was thinking and was too afraid to say aloud.

Maureen could be cruel, but so were other girls, though in a different way. It seemed more of a texture of their personalities than an attitude toward anything in particular, as if they'd grown thorns under their skin. One by one, somewhere along the way, all of these girls had learned to strike first. Denver suspected most Fours had learned this lesson, and so their fights were bitter and enduring, and all the girls united around one common enemy.

"My husband told me he'd give me a tanning if I didn't do...you know...that Sunday thing with him again on Wednesday! After thirteen hours at the nail salon!"

"Do that when he asks again and keep it in your pocket for later. My husband got mad yesterday, and I thought he might hit me, and then I said if he laid a finger on me, then I'd report it. Next time I'm going to record him begging. Why refuse it when you can use it?"

"How can you even stand it? We tried it once, and it hurt worse than getting socked. Now I just click Completed when the thing flashes."

Denver had to ask about this one. "You click without actually doing it? How?"

The girl shrugged, as if she hadn't really understood the question, or else didn't want to think about it. "Just do."

"But aren't you afraid you'll get a behavior audit? Your citizenship score could get severely downgraded."

The girl shrugged again, and Maureen leaned over and gave

Denver a look beneath a lowered brow that Denver took to mean *you'll never get through to them*. She turned away, but Maureen's eyes remained.

The instructor for this class was a Three, as instructors of everything were, although this particular Three must have been at the bottom of her class. Miss Tanenbalm wore earrings shaped like animals, frequently misspelled words she wrote on the screen, and peppered her speech with misused phrases like *could care less*. Denver imagined her as the kind of woman who spent her free time drinking alcohol with her friends, as only Threes and above were allowed to do, and exasperatedly talking about how her students weren't getting the material—for all of her concern and hard work.

"Girls," she was saying now, "let's set our focus for the day. Everyone together now!"

In a hushed, slurred chorus, the women read the words Tanenbalm had written above her own head.

"By five p.m. on August 11, the newly married will be able to define household finances (*fainances*), articulate the purpose of a joint account, and recite their expenses and their withdraw dates."

Denver knew she should be projecting a screen and copying these words down on her watch—Tanenbalm never kept the words projected for long, and now that Denver no longer received focus injections, she noticed her attention span was shortening. After she had a baby, she'd get to resume the injections—Metrics just didn't want them interfering with pregnancy, and the possibility was always looming now that she was married.

Tanenbalm smiled, and Denver caught a fleck of pink lipstick on her teeth. "Wonderful, girls. It's exactly four now, so let's get started if we're going to learn all this by five! Let's start with a warm up. Tell your partner which bank you and your husband use. Go."

There was a pause as the girls turned to their partners and silently negotiated who would speak first. Denver turned to Maureen, who rested her chin on her hand, not seeming to care that this pushed her skin up and distorted her face. Denver spoke first.

"We use People's United."

Maureen sighed. "We *all* use People's United."

There was half a moment of silence. Tanenbalm hadn't provided any further instructions for conversation, and her back was now to the group. Most of the women could be heard moving on to personal discussions.

In a low voice, Maureen said, "We would never have had off-topic conversations if we were in *our* class."

Denver wondered if she meant class in society or the marriage class for Threes. Stephen seemed nice enough, but she couldn't help but long for her old rank. Life as a Four didn't seem so bad when you were a Three, but now that Denver was here, she knew her old classification was chock full of little luxuries, like instructors who probably knew what they were talking about. Denver felt a familiar surge of panic, the kind that only comes when finding yourself amid the consequences of a past mistake. Why had she applied for marriage? Of course she was paired with a Four! It wasn't that she deluded herself into thinking she'd be matched with a Three; it just seemed like being a Four wouldn't be so bad. And if she was going to be honest, she really hadn't thought about it all that much. In the silence of her mind, she bitterly reprimanded herself over her own excitement for stepping into the unknown.

Maureen let out an *if you can't beat 'em* sort of breath. "Why are you here?"

"I got married."

"No, I mean, why are you a Four now?"

"Oh." Denver looked down at her pencil and paper where she'd begun to copy the focus but had given up when she remembered they never reached it by the end of the hour. "I have a brother."

"Oo-oh." Maureen's eyes got big. "Naughty mommy."

"She was going to have an abortion, but she said she got to the doctor and couldn't go through with it. It happens sometimes. You just have to make a lot of sacrifices if that's your choice."

"Like putting your first-born in a class full of...you know..." Maureen made a gesture Denver had never seen before.

Some of the girls quieted and gave over-the-shoulder glances to Denver and Maureen. Denver's cheeks warmed.

"They never went to high school, Maureen. They had to start work when they were twelve and they only spend time with people who—"

"Are uneducated too. Exactly." Maureen finished her sentence for her and smiled.

Denver realized Maureen thought she was agreeing. "They're not morons."

"No, no, of course not."

"Why are *you* here?"

Maureen groaned. "Bad citizenship score."

Tanenbalm turned back around and gave instructions, but Maureen was still talking in her low voice. "I didn't know it, but I was connected to someone who had participated in an organized protest against Metrics. They found out, and everyone who was connected to him was deducted just enough points to knock us down one class. My husband and I were both connected to this guy. But we can build that score back up, if we want, in the next few years."

"Maureen Short, can you recite the focus for the day?"

The words were no longer hanging in the air. *She's trying to embarrass her.* Denver was just regretting her choice to stop copying it down when Maureen, speaking as if she were on stage, lifted her chin and said, "By five p.m. on August 11, the newly married will be able to define household finances, articulate the purpose of a joint account, and recite their expenses and their withdraw dates."

Tanenbalm was visibly annoyed. "I could care less if you have an off-topic conversation, Miss Short. Just try to do it when I'm not talking."

———

That night, as Stephen's watch made those irritating, jolly noises next to her in bed, Denver looked at her own watch, scrolled absentmindedly, and wondered vaguely if she'd been too hard on Mom for her indiscretions. Before she knew it, she was typing in Samara's number. Samara's face appeared before her, along with the usual stats—height, weight, profession, interests... She clicked on Location as a matter of habit. It was always interesting to know where people were at the moment you were thinking of them.

According to the graph in front of her, Samara was at the edge of town, just on the outside of the fifth ring road. With her was a small yellow dot used to denote an unregistered person. Mostly these dots moved around, picking up trash or sweeping the floors. But this one stayed with her.

That was the first thing that made her angry that night. The second was when she woke up in the middle of the night after a startling dream where Samara had been destroying Bristol's work, throwing bricks at murals on walls and slowly chipping away the image he'd created. When she woke, the muscles around her eyes were already tight with fury. She tried relaxing them, but they only tightened again when she looked beside her and realized the bed was strangely cold. Stephen was gone.

CHAPTER NINETEEN

SAMARA HADN'T TASTED A BLACKBERRY IN EXACTLY SEVEN YEARS. On the last day of secondary school, the administrative staff had brought them in and passed them around to the students at the end of their last exam. She could still remember the bewildered look on her instructor's face as the tiny purple cups circulated around the room. Everyone's cup sat on their desks, and Samara studied it carefully, not moving her folded hands from the desk. Never before had she seen a fruit so small. Samara and her classmates had eaten apples, bananas, even a small orange once, but never a berry. The administration looked at the class, looking at their treats, before saying, "Begin!" Samara had hesitated, watching the teachers as her classmates began eating, making sure she was not out of bounds. Then she, like many students, took the entire remaining ten minutes to examine and savor every sour, juice-filled pocket.

Seven years later, it was still a favorite memory to call upon in bitter moments. Samara opened her eyes when she heard the mechanical lock being unhitched, and the memory faded as the large red door creeped open.

Before yesterday afternoon, Samara had been convinced there was no good reason to break a rule. She'd been trying to recall the last time she'd done it, but had yet to remember an instance in her life that she knew a rule and had deliberately broken it. That was the problem, they said, with people of the past; there was too much gray, not enough black and not enough white. Now everything was clear. There were hundreds of thousands of federal laws, so people knew that everything from intentionally splashing in a pool to chewing gum loudly in public was illegal. Everyone was taught and drilled on exactly what to say in response to most conversational phrases so no feelings were ever hurt. When she was a child and didn't know all the laws yet, she innocently broke a few, but never had something like this ever happened. Never had a child ever asked her to smuggle powder out of a prison. She did not recall that particular law, but she knew it must be one of them.

A guard was waiting for her on the other side of the door.

"Sorry, ma'am," the guard said offhandedly as she called back to the boys. "Move it."

Samara stood aside until the boys passed. At the end of the row was Warden Paul. She did not follow the boys but looked at Samara. The corners of her mouth turned up, though her eyes did not change.

"Miss Shepherd. Good morning."

"Good morning."

"I'd like to help you set up your classroom today."

She did not reach for either of Samara's two bags, weighing heavily on both shoulders, but walked beside her toward the cafeteria. Halfway there, she stopped and addressed a boy Samara didn't know—he must not have had school privileges—with a bathroom pass in his hands.

"Looking forward to your hearing next week, James. You have a bright future ahead of you, young man," Warden Paul said.

James beamed and looked at the floor, but Paul didn't notice. She was already barreling ahead, continuing toward the cafeteria.

Once there, Samara hefted both her bags onto a table still littered with breakfast dishes. The warden began unpacking the independent work packets and placing them down on the table.

Samara looked as Paul placed Timothy's book on Marcus's place, Marcus's book on Jamari's place, and so on.

"Miss Shepherd, we haven't yet discussed this, but you're a smart girl. You must realize that the boys here are...troubled."

Samara wanted to ask her what she meant, but the warden was already going on.

"Troubled in many ways. Many will have no chance at citizenship their entire lives, though they're probably not aware of it. Studies show that hope can be a wonderful source of energy."

"Oh? I—"

"Wonderful for productivity. But there's another side to this, Miss Shepherd. And I tell you this to prepare you, not to frighten you." The warden turned down her chin and lifted her brow. "The hope can sometimes make the boys do and say and think silly things. If they've committed any infractions inside our facility, for example, they can try to cover those up. And worse, convince the others to help them." The warden stopped here and looked expectedly at Samara.

"What kind of infractions, Warden?"

"All sorts. Degrees of seriousness. We had one boy stuff wads of toilet paper down the pipes to make the toilets overflow. Then he convinced every inmate to confess to it. Every one. But we caught that one...in the end."

"How?"

"I'm so glad you asked." Her eyes glistened. "What's your first guess? How did we catch him?"

"Oh...I don't know."

"Guess."

"The cameras?"

"Wrong! This was before our renovations. The cameras were easily disarmed. Even now, they can't catch everything. Guess again."

"I...don't know."

"You give up too quickly. Guess."

"He turned himself in?"

"In a way that's exactly what happened." The warden looked

slightly disappointed. "In the end, he felt he could trust one of our guards here and told her exactly what had happened. But what really clinched it was when the other boys came forth with the same story. They had hope."

"Hope for what?"

The warden said nothing, but grinned. "Miss Shepherd, surely you've noticed a common theme among the young women who work here. You yourself share this trait."

"I don't understand, Warden."

"Don't be modest. And maybe you've noticed you're not as relaxed as you used to be?"

Samara blinked. "My focus injections."

"Yes. Without them, you're experiencing the full range of female hormone levels. Somehow the boys can tell. It was only a decade ago that we realized if we employed young women with objective attractiveness as guards and let them experience their natural methods of manipulation, it would add to the illusion of hope that makes it possible for us to have excellent control over our young charges. Take away their focus injections, and biology does the work for us. It's very easy to modify behavior through hope. Doesn't work on girls, though. Girls are calculating. They like to imagine the exact circumstances and then formulate a plan to see it through. Luckily for us, boys aren't that sophisticated. They see a pretty girl, imagine an outcome, and then they leave themselves open.

"Give them hope. Schedule their hearings, tell them about their great promise, and surround them with pretty women they feel they can trust. Doesn't take much else for this place to run smoothly. So here's what you really need to know, Miss Shepherd: they need to trust you. And you need to trust me.

"I know what you're thinking: what's in it for me?" Warden Paul paused again and smiled. "I have an offer for you, Miss Shepherd. I don't usually let the instructors in on it, but I believe you deserve it."

Samara only glanced up cautiously, knowing the warden wouldn't let her speak even if she tried.

"Our guards get a little bonus every time they alert me to a potential infraction. If it's determined an infraction was definitely stopped by a guard, that bonus is not so small. You'll have the same privileges from here on."

"Thank you."

"When this place runs smoothly, life is good for all of us. Staff, inmates, stakeholders."

"Stakeholders?"

"The owners of our little operation. They're *Ones*." Her eyes shone with admiration. "Have a nice day, Miss Shepherd." She turned to leave. Then she paused and looked over her shoulder. "Forgot. If it's seen that you have, for some reason, kept an infraction to yourself, you will be punished."

There was a long pause.

"Any questions?"

"No." It came out slightly quieter than she'd expected. "Yes, I mean yes, but it's off topic."

"Please. I have about two more minutes."

"Where did those boys go? The ones in the line. I sometimes see a few boys get ready to leave, but then I don't see them again." Samara was no longer looking at the warden but at the wall behind her.

"Happily, those boys were found innocent of their crimes and were set free." She said it flippantly, with the same tone she'd used with James. "Can't have too many occupants in a prison, can we? That would probably mean something wasn't working correctly at the law-making level. It's easier to let boys go than to change laws. Have a nice day." And with that, she went through the wide doorway with no door, leaving Samara alone in the room, plates clattering while the silent kitchen staff continued cleaning up breakfast. Somehow the stench never left that room.

CHAPTER TWENTY

IT SEEMED TO JUDE THAT KOPECKY HAD DONE THE IMPOSSIBLE. For months, the other boys had told him there was no way he could be free, no matter what Mr. Richards said. Warden Paul, on the other hand, talked of appeals and of shortened sentences—the stuff of hope—and today, it seemed she was the one he could believe.

Kopecky had nearly wet himself with excitement when he told Jude his appeal had gone through. After all these years, he'd finally be free to join his mother and father outside the Fox County Detention Center's walls. In a matter of months, Kopecky had become Jude's only friend, so the news had stirred mixed emotions. Jude counted down the days leading to this one, doing his best to match Kopecky's excitement while privately wondering what he was going to do here without him. Sure, Miss Shepherd was an ally, and Jude still couldn't believe what she'd done for him, but Kopecky was the one he could really talk to. Kopecky had no way to know how terrible Jude was at kickball and algebra and flirting with girls, like the kids at Jude's old school had. They all hated him for that, fearing, maybe, that befriending him would someday cause citizenship points to be subtracted from their own records. But Jude thought even if Kopecky did know, he wouldn't have cared. And he liked that about prison—there was no score to worry about. Jude and Kopecky could be cross-tier friends. In the first light of morning, Jude was beginning to acknowledge his greatest fear: that his new life in prison had been better than his life outside, thanks in large part to his friend's kindness and openness. Without him, his life would go back to being lonely, his days long, his mind restless.

Kopecky's head popped out from the top bunk. "Today's the day!"

Jude smiled in spite of himself. "You're gonna set off the cameras!"

"A couple more hours and they can't touch me!" Kopecky whispered with a little more boldness before disappearing into his bed again.

The anthem blared immediately, irreverently piercing the still morning, and the overhead lights followed with a flicker. Jude watched his friend land with both feet on the cold concrete floor, throw his stiff white blanket on the bed again, and start dressing for the day all in a matter of seconds. Jude had to stop himself from begrudging thoughts. He wouldn't be missed. Of course not. What right did Jude have to be missed? He was, after all, associated with this terrible place. And Kopecky was headed for a life far from here, if not physically, then otherwise. Sure, he would be unregistered in his new life, but he had parents somewhere who would take care of him. He'd sleep in his own room, shower with hot water, and talk with people who loved him.

Jude wanted to be in Kopecky's new life with him, but there was no date set for him. Not yet, anyway. When he'd mentioned this to Kopecky, he said, "It's like what Warden Paul always says—there's always hope."

"Do you trust the warden?" Jude had asked, lowering his voice and his gaze.

"Yeah. She's a good lady. I heard she was a Five and got this job because she worked so hard. Don't know what you got against her."

That last bit was really meant to be a question, Jude knew, but he was still having trouble putting the incident with the bag together in his mind, still waiting for everything to unravel. It had definitely seemed the warden had set him up, but he couldn't prove anything, and things had been quiet in the weeks since. Still, even though Warden Paul seemed to be right about the eventual chance of freedom, something unseen told Jude she was not to be trusted. He wrestled with telling this to Kopecky, but he seemed so genuinely happy, and genuine happiness had become such a luxury that Jude couldn't kill it.

The boys finished getting ready and stood on their marks beside their bunks for inspection. The cool blonde guard waited patiently for the automated glass door to lower, and there was the daily collective inhale as the boys took in her perfume. Even Jude felt refreshed and ready at the first encounter of that warm, sweet scent. This morning, the unnamed guard locked eyes with Kopecky.

"Good morning."

"G'morning, ma'am."

"Kopecky?"

"Yes, ma'am?"

"I look forward to escorting you into the outside world today."

The boys had stopped breathing. The guard was unfazed, still looking into Kopecky's stunned face. Usually guards had simple greetings and one-word commands for them, like *Walk*, *Stop*, and *Eat*, but this was the first time they'd ever heard a full sentence. It gratified Jude in a way he could not explain. As for Kopecky, he made a motion with his tongue that might have been "th," but could not go any further. The guard smiled and continued her inspection lazily. "Good!" she confirmed before leaving their cell again.

The boys looked toward the far left bunk incredulously.

"How d'y'like that!" Kopecky's smile was so radiant that no one could resist matching it.

Kopecky was still there at lesson time, in his usual seat. They weren't supposed to talk here, but it was only Miss Shepherd and no guards, so the hall was alive with the ambient buzz of conversations as she passed out books.

"You're still here!"

His signature grin appeared. "Until noon, buddy boy."

"Lucky."

"Yeah. Well..." He scratched his head. "You know I been here since I was five. That's a long time."

"Ten years."

"Yeah, genius, ten years." The shape of a smirk lingered on his otherwise thoughtful face. "I don't even really remember what it is to be outside, to tell the truth. And you know what I was thinking today? This morning? Y'ain't never asked me what I done to get in here to start with."

It was true. Selfishly, Jude did not want to think of Kopecky as dangerous. What if he'd done something horrible, like injure or kill someone? But he didn't want to know if he was innocent either. Knowing two innocent people locked up here—maybe more—would be too depressing to process. Months after meeting him, Jude still did not want to know. He shrugged.

"I never told nobody the whole truth about this, but I'm gonna tell you." He looked left and right and then back at Jude. "Nothing. Didn't do a damn thing."

Jude's stomach sank. So it was true. He was probably just in the wrong place at the wrong time, just like himself.

"My parents did, though. They were in the Red Sea."

"The Red Sea?" Jude's voice was too loud, and several boys turned their heads to look.

"Shh! They don't need no advertising!" He lowered his chin. "It's a group that tried to change the way things are. Let everyone have a say in the way things are done. Let people do whatever they want—choose their jobs, their wife, where they live—just as long as they don't hurt nobody, let 'em be. That's what I heard, anyway. Like I said, I don't remember much. They had meetings at our house every now and then where they talked about things. I remember my mom telling people they had to be brave and stand up for what they believed in, and I remember people waving their hands at her. It was a secret meeting and they were trying to be quiet. That's what they did when they liked something, they waved their hands."

Kopecky was looking behind Jude's face now, past cafeteria workers wiping up the last crumbs of breakfast.

"Metrics came to take them on my fifth birthday. That I remember, 'cause we had a cake with chocolate icing, and I still had some on my mouth when they busted down the door. My mom screamed and reached for me, and my dad just looked at me square in the face and said, 'We'll see you soon.' And I cried and screamed too, all the way here. Tasted the salt from my tears mixed with that icing. I tell you, I've thought about that so many times, what my dad said. 'See you soon.' I never thought this day would come. The warden told me, though, that they're coming to pick me up. So we all musta been let out on the same day."

Jude cleared his throat. "That's really good to hear."

"Yeah. Have you heard the 'A hundred come, three go' rule?"

He had. A rumor had circulated among the boys that when a hundredth inmate was added to the roster, that's when three existing inmates were finally cleared. It did seem to make sense, though Jude would always forget to keep track exactly of how many boys were coming in, and he had no proof anyway in such a big place.

Kopecky leaned in. "It's bullshit." He paused and relished the curse for a moment. "See, today's my birthday. It's been ten years. I never knew this, but that's gotta be the sentence they made us all do. Exactly ten years. It all makes sense."

Without warning, a warmth came to Jude's eyes. "Happy Birthday, buddy."

"You crying?" Kopecky delivered a good-natured punch on Jude's arm. "Not me. I'm gonna eat real birthday cake today—no added salt!"

Miss Shepherd had been trying to start the lesson for the past few minutes, and now seemed as good a time as any to help her. As their conversation quieted, many others followed suit. Miss Shepherd looked relieved that she could finally stop saying, "Class?" and teach them how to sound out four-letter words. Jude listened with a new energy, truly glad for Kopecky's departure.

The doors opened and a guard stepped through. "Kopecky, Albin."

He stood. The guard turned her head to see him.

"Come."

He reached his long legs over the bench and left with a wink, taking his flimsy notebook with him. The rest of the lesson progressed without any further disruption. When the blessed bell rang, the boys took their usual places in line as four guards filed in to escort them back. Jude waited until his teacher was close.

"Miss Shepherd? I saw that some words have a coupla consonants at the beginning. How would you know which one to say?"

The guard closest to him let out a snicker.

After a moment of hesitation, she turned to the guard. "I'll take him and explain before my next lesson. I'll walk him to his work area myself. Is that all right?"

The guard shrugged. "Sure."

"Sit down, Reeder." Samara nodded to the bench closet to the front, and he obediently sat with his hands folded.

"So there are two types of words with double consonants at the beginning. The first type is a blend, and that's where you say both the sounds very quickly together to make one sound, like *flit*." The last of the boys walked out of the room, and a hushing puff of air signaled the close of the door. "There's an *F* and an *L* and you say them together and—" They were all gone. "Okay, what is it?"

"Thank you. For before."

Samara smiled and breathed in more deeply. "Of course. Any more insight into who did it or why?"

"I don't know anything. I thought maybe Warden Paul had something to do with it, but she doesn't."

Samara shifted in her seat. "How do you know?"

"Kopecky trusts her. And I trust him. And I've been thinking, maybe this isn't so bad. I've been scared for a long time that something wasn't really right here, but I'm thinking now everything's gonna be okay. I'm going to get out when I'm supposed to, just like Kopecky."

"Just keep your head low and try to get through your sentence, Jude. They're worried their genetic matching didn't work with you. You've got to go out of your way to show them you're..." Jude could see she was searching for a word. Smarter? Stronger? Better? "You've just got to try harder."

Jude lowered his head. This speech sounded familiar. "Yes, ma'am."

"I should probably get you back to your work area. There's another class coming in ten minutes." She followed his gaze toward the kitchen, where leftover English muffins formed a stack on the counter. "Are you hungry?"

He nodded. "They've taken my meals. Until I confess."

Miss Shepherd gave him a strange look; was it pity? Most adults fresh from the you're-not-living-up-to-your-potential lecture were angry at him by the end of it, but she didn't seem to be. "They're going to throw those out anyway. Let's go get just one."

They walked to the kitchen. Just as they'd crossed the wide threshold, the automatic door made its familiar *pffffffst*. Someone was coming into the cafeteria on the other side. The two hit the floor, and Samara opened the door to a large cupboard, which was mercifully empty and spacious.

"In here," she mouthed.

From inside the cupboard, a small crack between the doors allowed them to see the rest of the room. A guard marched in first, followed by two other older boys. Why were they still here? Kopecky was taken from class a half an hour ago, at least. Sure enough, as the line proceeded and came to a halt, Kopecky himself stopped in the middle of the room. He was carrying something in his hands—a piece of black folded fabric. All the boys carried the same item. A parting present, maybe?

"Turn!" The voice of the warden, unseen but unmistakable, boomed from somewhere in the cafeteria. "Thank you. Shortly, you will all be taken to our family receiving center, where your families are waiting for you. I myself have just come from there, and I can say that they are truly anxious to see you. The room is filled with balloons, signs, cake"—Kopecky's eyes shined—"and other welcome-home goodies. We have just one more step to complete, and you will be on your way.

"As you may or may not know, there have been some diseases in the past few years on the outside that you have been protected from, living here in safety. The flu has been especially rampant. For your own protection, we'll first give you a vaccine, a Band-Aid in the color of your choice, and then we'll get back on the bus and send you on your way. This is a high dose of the vaccine, so you may feel dizzy or nauseous, but only for a few minutes. Don't be alarmed. Please pull up your right shirtsleeve."

The boys obeyed. From their hiding place, Jude and Samara saw Kopecky push up his sleeve, stick out his arm, and wait for his injection as eagerly as if he were anticipating a kiss. The guards—three of them, one for each boy—injected the skin above their forearms. Some gasped. Kopecky coughed and murmured, "She wasn't kidding 'bout the nausea thing! Feels like I could..."

He drifted off, and coughed again through his teeth, trying his best to laugh it off. Next to him, a boy dropped to the ground. His guard took the black fabric from his lifeless hand, shook it out so it became a bag, and swiftly stuffed his body inside. Kopecky was still coughing, so forcefully now that it was taking all his concentration. Jude had the intense desire to do something crazy and brave, like run into the room, punch the guard in her perfectly shaped nose, and carry Kopecky away, but he stayed hidden, immobile and horrified.

Jude and Samara saw him drop. They saw his guard take the black bag. And they saw his face disappear behind it, the corners of his mouth—perhaps still expecting to soon be stained with icing—still upturned.

The warden exhaled loudly. "Not a pretty sight, ladies, but necessary. We've got another one scheduled for tomorrow, then that should be all for quite a while after that. Metrics is finally taking steps to remove all the unregistered, so we'll have less incoming inmates."

"Remove, Warden?" asked one of the guards.

"I've been told that for the unregistered removal, the police will use these same injections." She held an empty syringe up to the light. "It's a very humane method. Quick and painless."

"Who is scheduled for tomorrow, Warden?"

Jude's breath stopped in his throat.

"Number 17201, of course. The Reeder child. I don't think he'll confess before tomorrow, but we'll give him a last meal anyway."

CHAPTER TWENTY-ONE

FACES WERE ALWAYS HARD FOR BRISTOL. CLOSING HIS EYES FOR the thousandth time, he tried to visualize the ratio between her cheekbone and the bottom corner of her eye. He'd just seen her the night before, unbelievably lovely and disarming in her own room.

Thoughts of Samara dominated Bristol's mind. Over and over, he recalled how the moon had come out from behind the clouds when he'd beckoned him up her fire escape, which felt like good luck. Bristol was incessantly superstitious. It drove his family crazy, but he'd never made an effort to change. The forgotten wisdom of looking for guiding signs was too alluring to ignore. Besides, even if Samara knew the innocent boy personally, there was no way she could know who was behind the graffiti. And he'd never tell her— just in case.

This morning, he had easily drawn those arms, that body, but still had trouble with her face. It was maddening, being able to see her in his mind's eye but not being able to capture it. He'd already drawn her rocking horse ten different times.

He wouldn't be able to finish it today. He was already going to risk being late for work. Another ten or so hours of chopping onions and cleaning pans and generally being one of those underlings who higher tiers so depended on to keep up their lifestyle. Bristol had spent years with bitter, scathing thoughts toward the proprietor of the restaurant—and ultimately Metrics. Stealing his time on earth for their own gain. As he grew older, he saw the wisdom in Denver's advice: "There's nothing you can do to change it, so don't think about it too much. Just show up, and rely on something else to make you happy." For Denver, that had been games on her watch. Watching her eyes glaze over on the couch when she played, Bristol was mostly secretly glad he wasn't allowed one.

But circumstances change. It was ridiculous to even think about. Now he found himself wishing he did have one—and a number. Then he could apply for a spouse. He knew it was crazy, that you had no control over who you married. The odds that you knew the right person for you were surely so slim that of course most people met their spouses on their wedding day. He turned his hopes to the next best thing—that Samara would not decide to apply for a spouse and they could continue to see each other every now and then. It was the best he could hope for.

And he didn't mind doing that little favor for her. In fact, he hoped he'd have another opportunity tonight.

The prep kitchen was loud today, though no louder than usual. It always took a minute or two to adjust and hear one's own thoughts again. A radio played rock music, which mostly sounded like crashing cars, and over that a projected news anchor's head blared. Through the noise, Bristol calmed his own movements, gently taking his apron down from the nail it hung on and tying it tenderly around his body.

"But *why* are these people so dissatisfied? Have we not given them a job? Have we not allowed them to live in this society?"

Another prep cook, the same who'd received a warning about talking, glanced at Bristol and lowered his chin. "They talkin' about us."

Bristol turned off the radio. The prep cook's face took on an expression of surprise and then gratitude. An aggravated voice from the news was all that could be heard now.

"These people—these *unregistered*—they are a burden on society. I'm sick of all this 'they're the strength of the nation' crap. The fact is that in a country where we now have to make up jobs for the Ones and the Twos, we could do better. Give those unregistered jobs to the Fives, let the Fours do the jobs of the Fives, and so on. We'd all have more if these unregs didn't drain our resources!"

"If you're just joining us now, we're talking about the implementation of a new effort to reorganize society, many calling for the removal of so-called 'unregs'—that's unregistered citizens—and relocating them so there are more resources for the documented citizens. Of course, this idea has been around for years—decades, even—but today, Metrics took a bold step in removing the first 100,000 unregs, relocating them to the western desert states.

"We just heard from a top policy maker saying, essentially, fewer people means society doesn't have to spread its resources so thin, meaning the quality of life rises for all documented people, especially if they're in the top tiers."

"That *is* what I'm saying, Shara," the man in the suit continued. "We've got too many people. We tried to fix this three decades ago with the single-responsibility policy—"

"In which families were allowed only one child."

"Yes"—he balked at being interrupted—"but as I argued at that time as well, the policy didn't go far enough. Women need sterilization after their one child. They cannot be trusted to have one baby and report for their injections with perfect timing after that."

"Sometimes—rarely, but it has happened—the injections don't work."

"Yes! Exactly!" The man was nearly choking with enthusiasm. "Technology fails us, people fail us, and if we're going to have a correct society, one in which everyone has enough and no one wants for anything, we need to protect ourselves against failure. Fewer people to drain us. Get the unregs out and make sure we don't get any more."

Bristol and the prep cook exchanged glances. They both went

back to their vegetables. With his eyes firmly on the carrots, Bristol spoke first, each word carefully measured.

"Where is everyone else?"

"We the only ones here today. They didn't have enough room for me on the bus. Boss is listening to the news in the office."

He wanted to reach out and touch him somehow—a hug, a pat on the back, anything—but was aware, as ever, of the cameras pointed down at their movements, ready to betray them if they stopped chopping. The anchors were still talking, but the sound was a nasal train passing by now. They were saying nothing, just continuing to complain about the wants in their lives and blaming people they didn't know because of it.

Bristol pressed the garbage down into the bag and tied it. He walked out the back door and swung the sack over his head and into the dumpster, trying his best not to breathe in the sickly sweet air that never left this courtyard.

"Psst."

His first thought was that it was a mouse—the soft sound had to be an animal. He looked down and around and heard it again.

"Psst. Bristol."

A shadow darkened Samara's copper face. She stood beside the building, behind a ladder with vines wrapped around the rungs. Though the situation didn't look good, he couldn't stop a small smile.

"What are you doing here?" he asked.

"Keep working. Pull some leaves off the ladder to make it look like you're busy."

Bristol obeyed, taking leaves down to the right of Samara and tossing them in the dumpster. "Listen—we have to get out of here. Have you heard what they're trying to do to the unregs?"

"They say that every couple of years. It's fine."

"This is different," she whispered. "They're taking the unregs now. And they won't relocate you. They'll kill you."

Bristol's heart thumped. "What? No."

"You know it's true. And I definitely know it's true. I saw the warden kill three boys today. I saw it with my own eyes. Have you seen the news today?"

Bristol had never seen this kind of fever in a person's eyes. He wished he had a pencil and paper and the courage to tell her to stand still. "Yes..."

"Then you know they're rounding up the unregistered. It's time to move, but we're going to make a pit stop at Fox. We'll break out a boy living there. They're all in danger really, but he's in the deepest. And then we'll go."

"Where are we going?"

"North." Her eyes widened as she leaned away from the shadow. "We can live there. There are farms with safe houses for unregs."

Bristol couldn't believe what he was hearing. "Live there? What are you talking about? I've got family here. Metrics isn't going to just kill us."

"Oh, then what? They'll relocate you? You still won't be with your family. And sorry for the spoiler, but you won't be living in Arizona or wherever. You'll be dead. I wish I didn't know that, but I do. Now are you coming with me, or do I have to break this little boy out of prison myself and take him to up north alone?"

The whole thing sounded so crazy that Bristol didn't know where to start. Even if they knew where they were going, how would they get there? He had no idea how far it was, but he knew it was at least a couple hours in a car, which none of them knew how to drive. Then there was his chip, and Samara's watch—surely they would have implanted a chip in the boy as well by now. It was in the vein in Bristol's wrist, meant to leave him to bleed to death if he ever tried to cut it out. He didn't think it worked anymore, but what if it did? He couldn't keep ice on it for that long.

"Samara, it sounds like you haven't quite worked out the details. And I promised my sister I'd stop with the sneaking around. This seems like the time to make good on that."

"It's already in motion. I put my watch in a bag of rocks and dropped it in the river on the way here. Do you hear those sirens? They're for me. They're looking for my body in the water."

As if by magic, he did hear them wailing in the air. He shivered.

"The battery has already been damaged, so they won't find my watch. They'll have moved on to looking for my body. If they find the watch though, we're in bigger trouble, so we have to move. I'm sorry to have to do this, but the time has come for me to help you. Are you coming?"

The sirens continued singing their song of panic. He looked at Samara for the first time since he heard her calling to him and saw tiny orbs of sweat shining on her forehead. His own shirt grew damp.

"No. I can't."

"It was nice knowing you, Bristol."

"Samara—" What could he say? He was sorry? He didn't want to believe she was right. He wanted to trust in the system that had always kept him down but safe. At least he always knew where he stood. But he thought of her little student, how he had been caught for Bristol's crime, how the child was still behind bars, how he'd never told her the truth.

It was too late to think through any of this with her, of course. She was gone.

CHAPTER TWENTY-TWO

IN AN IDEAL WORLD, SAMARA WOULD HAVE TAKEN HER TIME formulating a plan to get Jude out. She may have even asked Jude himself for his opinion. He seemed bright, and although she didn't consider herself stupid, she wasn't as good in these think-on-your-feet situations. She'd hoped at least Bristol would help, although that hope had fizzled fast. Bitter thoughts of good riddance clouded her mind, and she worked to clear them. She needed all her brainpower. *No distractions tonight.*

Just one obstacle would have provided enough difficulty, but there were three. The cameras, ever present in every room in almost every angle; the chip, tracking his every movement; and herself. She was supposed to be dead right now, and she didn't know whether the night guards would have that information. There was only one way into Fox Juvenile Detention Center, and that was the way she intended to go. She could only hope that in all the hubbub, no one would have thought to inform her employer.

She pressed the Call button on the front door and waited. It was seconds, or minutes, but sometimes time is different, unmeasured in such terms. She only knew she waited long enough to hear her heartbeat in her ears.

"Hello?" said a cool and clear female voice at the other end of the line.

"Hello! Sorry to bother you, but my watch isn't letting me in today. I think I need to get something checked, but could you let me in for now? I forgot something in the cafeteria."

"Oh, sure."

And then she was walking down the hallway she had gone through so many times before, though it suddenly felt strange and foreign. She had a vision of herself walking as if she were disconnected from her body. She walked past the cafeteria and, as if in a dream, walked straight into the warden's office, which, mercifully, was unlocked.

The lights were out, shading everything in the room in a dark yellow from the light outside the small window above Warden Paul's chair. She took a moment to scan the room clockwise, looking for controls for the cameras. She thought it was probably a stupid idea—the cameras would be controlled remotely from the warden's watch. If an emergency override system was in place, it would probably send a message alerting the warden to the change, giving Samara minutes to rescue Jude.

Like most people, Samara had no idea how technology worked, only how to use it if it was functioning perfectly. She had a vision of herself as a more prepared rescuer, fiddling with wires and rerouting the cameras, but this fantasy quickly vanished as she assessed the tools she did have—an intercom and a contact list on the wall.

Warden Paul had gone home for the night, but possibly the night guards didn't know that. Without losing a second, she looked at the list of guards under the *NIGHT SHIFT* heading and called the first one.

Hearing the beep that meant the guard was being signaled, she cleared her throat and stood a little taller on the plush carpet next to the desk.

"Guard 2208 speaking."

"I need inmate 17201, Jude Reeder. Bring him to my office as soon as possible," Samara said in her deepest voice, doing her best to imitate the growl the warden used when speaking softly. As she did, she watched the cameras and saw that the guard speaking into her phone was alone. Small miracles.

"Yes, Warden."

Samara watched the guard click her phone off and walk toward Jude's cell. She noticed a second button beside the intercom and, thinking it might give the video some audio, pressed it. Immediately, a soft blue ray of light shot out, and a projection appeared on the wall behind her.

FOX COUNTY DETENTION CENTER DATABASE

A box appeared below. She half hoped it wouldn't work, but she reached over to the numerical keypad anyway and typed Jude's number. His picture immediately appeared, with his general information below it, and a little box all the way at the bottom labeled *Log*. She tapped it.

THREAT TO INMATES. Has been observed trying to modify behavior in dining hall.

"You saw it and modified the others' behavior yourself!" whispered Samara.

Attempts to dispatch:
July 7. Placed a bag of drift under bed. Bag disappeared. Suspect Albin Kopecky (966) assisted. Will place another in same location in six weeks. Will remove 966.

Samara's skin flamed and she wished she had her watch to take a picture. So it had been the warden. She quickly turned the lights on in the office and waited by the door. When she heard two sets of footsteps approaching, she opened it an inch.

"Thank you. I'll take him from here," Samara said. She looked over her shoulder at the empty chair. "He's here, Warden."

The guard hesitated. "She's in there?"

"She and I both came back tonight. It's an...emergency meeting. I don't think I can say any more. Come in, Jude." Samara looked at the guard. "Thank you."

The guard nodded and click-clacked down the hallway in her shiny black boots.

Inside the office, Samara whipped her head to face Jude. "We're getting out of here. Both of us. We're going north."

"Now?"

"Yes."

"What about my chip?"

"We're just going to have to run faster than they can keep up with us."

They looked into each other's hopeless eyes. It was impossible, and they both knew it. But on whose terms would they rather die?

Samara continued, "There's a garbage chute in the kitchen. I'll enter my ID manually to get in. Then we'll go down it. I think it goes outside to the dumpster. From there we'll be on foot."

"Okay."

"Act like you're in trouble."

Jude looked down at his feet and they walked out of the office and down the hallway to the cafeteria. Samara punched in her code and heard the door unlock.

They crossed the cafeteria, passed the long tables, and headed into the kitchen. Just as they crossed the threshold, they heard the door unlock again. Samara looked at Jude, and her face gave the command without saying a word: *Hide*.

Jude dashed into the same cupboard he'd watched Kopecky die from that morning, but thought better of that; he ran to the other end of the kitchen, closer to the chute, and unsheathed a kitchen knife from the counter before disappearing beneath it and closing the cupboard.

Samara kept her gaze locked on the door, where four guards were crossing the cafeteria and headed straight for her. She could think of nothing to do, so she breathed.

"Stay," one of them said. She cleared her throat. "Miss Shepherd, I trust you've found your book by now."

"Indeed. I'll get going." Samara began to move past them.

"Wait," said the same one, who seemed to have organized this mission. "Where is it?"

"What?"

"The book you forgot."

"I must have left it on the bus. I'll call the station in the morning."

The guard smiled. "Call them now."

"What?"

"Call them now. With your watch. We'll wait."

"I don't...I left it at home."

"No one leaves their watch at home, Miss Shepherd. Enough. Where is he?"

"Who?"

"The boy—17201. We know you took him here. Where is he?"

"I don't know."

"Liar! Somebody get me a signal on 17201."

Samara's heart sank. The chip. As their heads all turned down to their wrists, trying to race each other to the signal, she heard the subtle flap of the chute hit the wall. If anyone else heard it, they made no indication. None of their eyes had moved from their watches.

The tall guard was first to see the signal. She looked up from her watch toward the chute. "He's under the counter, over there."

All of them sprinted across the kitchen, including Samara. As she approached the chute, they crowded around the cupboard, and soon a shrill scream rang on the kitchen walls.

Just before launching herself down into the dumpster, she saw what had caused the sudden uproar. Inside the cupboard was a small severed hand lying in a pool of bright blood.

CHAPTER TWENTY-THREE

WITH EACH BIT OF CARROT ADDED TO THE PILE, BRISTOL'S CASE for running was building. He didn't want Samara to be hurt, which she surely would be, and then again, if he went with her, he surely would be too. Still, she'd thrown herself into harm's way for her student and for him. The way he felt about her was unlike anything he'd experienced before. It was like the feeling he felt for his mother and sister, and also unlike that feeling in every way. He needed her like he needed his family, and she was in danger. That might have been good enough for him after all, though he never got to test this theory.

The manager was screaming outside. Bristol distinctly heard the words "destroy my business" and "close today." He and the other prep cook looked at each other, though neither one of them could manage to stop slicing the carrots.

"I'm getting out of here," Bristol finally said. "Now. You coming?"

"I can't...what?"

Bristol dropped his knife on the cutting board. The stunned prep cook looked at the knife, at Bristol, and then back to the front door, where the manager could now be heard arguing louder.

"Let's go."

"They're here for us. They're going to take us to New Mexico."

"They will not. Are you coming or not?"

Bristol waited for an answer as long as he dared, but the way the knife moved in the prep cook's hands said it all. He couldn't stop, and he couldn't go. Bristol still wasn't certain his chip was activated but he could take no chances. He'd need his trusty ice-pack trick to get him to Samara. He ran into the walk-in freezer just as the police burst through the door, trailed, it sounded like, by the manager making his final, exasperated arguments.

"What about tomorrow? Am I supposed to lose *two* days of business?"

The door to the freezer was heavy steel. Although Bristol could hear his manager's cries clearly, the police officer's reply was faint.

"...transition for everyone... better in the end...bandage."

"Just tell me when they're coming back!"

"...relocated...two men?"

Bristol's cold breath rose above his face. He moved quietly to the side of the door.

"Where...other one?"

If it was possible to feel more of a chill, he felt it. In his mind's eye, he saw his coworker's hand put the knife down and point toward the freezer door. And what he heard next was the unmistakable sound of the door being locked from the outside. He heard the officer's next words clearly.

"Do not open this until tomorrow morning. We'll know if you do."

A few more words of protest from the manager, weaker this time, then silence. He was alone and locked in the freezer. Samara was right. They were killing the unregs.

Think, Bristol told himself. *Don't panic.* He breathed heavily to calm himself before realizing that was probably a bad idea given the limited oxygen. He looked around and gathered all the newspaper and plastic wrap he could find from around the vegetables. And threw them into an unsightly pile in the center of the freezer. When he could find nothing else, he stuffed these into his clothing and used the tape from the produce boxes to wrap his body. His new insulated suit wasn't much, but he hoped it would allow him to survive the day and night. He paced. If he were alive when the door finally did open, he realized, he would probably have to fight whomever was on the other side. He'd never been in a fight in his life, but he would have made it too far at that point to allow himself to be "relocated." He jabbed the frosty air a few times, wishing he'd brought his knife.

He shadowboxed until his breath came more heavily. Then he paced again, but slower. Practicing for that step to freedom would be of no use if he ran out of air in this cold metal box.

One hour passed, then two. He'd heard no voices for such a long stretch that he tried kicking the door open a few times, which he knew would be a failure from the start, yet only stopped when his suit began to unravel.

Sometime in the fifth hour, still pacing, he bit into an apple and remembered his midafternoon oatmeal. The apple suddenly became soft, hot mush in his mouth. He jerked his hand back toward his body and let the apple fall. He didn't hear it hit the floor. *Oxygen.* The thought seemed to drift by him. *Not enough. Get a grip.*

"You! Hey!"

A pair of man's hands were at his shoulders. Bristol remembered something about a fight and threw a groggy punch in the air. His fist landed limply by his side.

"Get him out of there first," came a woman's voice from the door. With great effort, Bristol raised his head. A woman he did not recognize walked toward him with a dark blue blanket.

"Help me with him."

She wrapped him in the blanket, and the heat from the wool gave him new life. They got him to his feet and guided him into the kitchen, where even in the dark, Bristol recognized the manager's face above his yellow tie.

"You made it. You son of a gun, I knew you would."

"I'm sorry we had to wait so long. You'll be all right." The woman put another blanket over his head as she spoke.

"This is my wife, Andi. What's your name?"

"Bristol." He looked up, hardly able to believe this was happening.

"Bristol! Four years of working with this kid and I finally get to know his name!" He spoke to his wife, who was busy inspecting Bristol's hands and feet. "My name is John. I doubt you knew that."

"No frostbite. Lucky kid."

Bristol didn't know where to start. "What's going on? Are the police here? What happened to the others?"

John and Andi looked at each other as if they were actors who'd forgotten their lines. John sighed. "Listen, I feel for you unregs. I always did. When it came time to open this place, I could have employed all registered workers, but I didn't. It's not what you think, either—I could have gotten a big tax break for hiring registered, so it's not like it comes out to be that much cheaper in the end. I felt sorry for your people. Metrics sends a letter once every few years to tell us businesses that employ you people to expect to lose our unregs soon. They sent one last week, but I didn't think nothing of it. Got them before, and nothing happened."

Andi kicked at the freezer door. "We have to break something," she explained. "We're going to tell them you broke out."

"It's broken enough. Can't make too much noise, hon."

"Right. Okay."

"Anyway, they came today and took most of my people here. Lucky you were late. That little rat you work with—I don't know his name—he told them you were in there! I can't believe it! What's the matter with people anymore, huh?"

"John," Andi said softly.

"Right. Too much noise. Well, I told my wife, 'That boy's worked hard for us for four years. Soon as curfew gets here, we're breaking that poor boy out.' Afraid what you do next is up to you, son."

"What if you get caught?"

"We will. But they won't care."

"What?"

"Believe it or not, I think my family will help me." Bristol wanted to ask what he meant, but his mouth still had to work hard to form words and John looked as though he wouldn't explain, anyway. "Don't worry about me, young man. It's not like you're a wanted criminal or anything. They won't care about one runaway unreg."

John and his wife chuckled. Bristol stretched his jaw wide as his mind slowly came back online. "I need a bag of frozen vegetables and a rubber band."

They were produced, and Bristol tied the vegetables to the back of his hand. He knew it wouldn't give him much time, but still, it was something. With a good-luck pat on the back and a promise from Bristol not to forget their kindness—or, thinking silently, the way he'd misjudged the man whose name was unknown to him for so many years—he was out the door again into the night, taking care to dart around the recorded streets.

CHAPTER TWENTY-FOUR

SAMARA THOUGHT OF HER FAMILY AS THEY WALKED. SHE'D LEFT A note under her dad's pillow. She didn't have her watch anymore and couldn't even tell the time... Jude told her he thought about nine by the position of the moon, and she'd believed him since he'd been in science classes more recently than she had. Her dad had probably found the note by now.

Dad,

I think you know what I've done. I love you
and I won't waste this chance.

Samara

P.S. You should burn this.

She'd assumed Dad had understood. At least now that Metrics considered her dead, they'd have to let Mom come back; he needed her much more than he needed Samara. She hoped the letter was in the incinerator. Still, hunger and exhaustion were pawing at her trust, and she wondered. Her father loved her, of course, but she remembered how people used to keep pets. They claimed they loved those, too, and so much that they needed to keep them in cages so they would always be around to love. She'd never considered this until now, of course. Her wet pants rubbed at her thighs, and her fingers swelled from swinging by her sides. Since she was registered, and hadn't done anything up to a few hours ago to provoke suspicion, her dad might think the police would treat her well. What would they say if he knew the details of what his daughter had done? He would know that Samara had totally screwed up any chance of a normal life after this, and all for a student and a friend. And what if his loneliness and desperation got the better of him? *Snap out of it. At least you've still got two hands.*

Fortunately, Jude also had first aid knowledge. Samara had found him outside the dumpster, standing next to a pond of his own vomit, but seemingly fine nonetheless, with a tourniquet around his wrist and the stump protruding from it. After they'd run for longer than they thought they could and walked for hours in silence, she'd asked about it, and he'd explained to her how it worked.

He'd had to put it on while the hand was still attached. The tourniquet, he explained, was a tool to stop bleeding in a limb, at the expense of that limb. When Samara still looked confused, he said, "Think of it this way. If I were bleeding from the wrist, I would put it on to stop losing too much blood. But then I'd still lose my hand."

Samara nodded. "When can you take it off?"

A corner of his nose moved up. "I don't think I can. It might release a blood clot to my heart."

She gently let go of a piece of brush so it wouldn't swat his face. "So you'll just keep it on?"

"I don't know what else to do."

"I'm sorry I don't have my watch. Maybe when we get to the safe house, they'll know what to do."

"When will we get there? Where is it?"

Impressed with the bravery Jude had shown tonight, she decided she didn't want to push him any further. She put on her mask of confidence and said, "Somewhere in Fallwood. I don't know exactly, but there'll be a sign and we'll see it."

"What's the sign?"

She hesitated, the snaps of twigs and leaves under her feet temporarily amplified. "Don't worry, Jude. We'll see it."

On they walked until Samara finally heard a sniffle, which provoked a tingling above her own nose, and she breathed deeply to stop it in its tracks.

"That was great running back there. Were you on the track team?"

Sniff. "No."

"You were phenomenal. And I can't believe you're still walking here, after seeing...after doing...what I'm trying to say, Jude, is that you're very brave, and I'm very brave, and I have to believe that good things come to people like us. What good would have come from sitting around? You saw what happened to..." She realized she could not say Kopecky's name.

"Yeah." He sounded stronger, and he was picking up his feet a little higher than before. "And anyway, Fallwood is only another ten miles away or so. We should get there before one, if we keep up the pace we're going now. I'm glad we're close."

She'd had no idea if it was so close, having looked only at city maps for most of her adult life. She hoped they were going in the right direction, but he probably would have said something by now if they were not.

So, on they walked, with conviction and purpose at first, and then a little more slowly when the adrenaline had run its course. Samara had heard of all sorts of things in these woods, wild animals and poisonous insects and hidden traps set by Metrics for rule-breakers such as themselves, yet if any of these were in the woods, then some higher power had, so far, guided them away from these threats. Samara felt it helped that they were walking carefully but

not timidly. Self-amputation and faking your own death had a way of
changing you.

Jude began stumbling when they were less than an hour from
Fallwood. Less than an hour was what he'd said, but she wasn't sure
whether or not she could trust that. He'd said it with a slur.

"Less juss keep goin'. Can we keep goin'?"

"No, let's stop for a moment. Let's lie down here—" No sooner
had the words left her mouth than she saw it. The first camera, or so
she hoped, fixed on a tall black pole in the midst of the trees. Jude
saw it too.

"We're not gonna makit."

"Of course we're going to make it, sweetheart. We just have to
walk around it."

"Thassa lasercam."

She froze. She'd heard of lasercams but had never seen one up
close. She helped Jude sit against a tree, found a thick stick, and used
what strength she had left to toss it in the path of the camera. A red
laser, perfectly positioned in the center of the stick, appeared as it
was still falling midair, and it was dust before it hit the ground. She
looked right and left. Of course they were lined up, all pointed
toward Fallwood.

Because she did not know what else to do, she laughed. "They
must pay high taxes for such security."

But Jude didn't answer. He was slumped unresponsive against
the tree.

"Jude? Are you okay?"

Nothing. He was still breathing, and there was a pulse in his
throat, but otherwise his body was silent, and now it seemed so very
small.

Less than an hour away. She had to believe it was true. *Don't
overthink it.*

"Listen," she whispered, "if you can hear me, please, just hold on.
If you've got anything left in you, use it to hold on to me."

Two options: over or under. Digging a tunnel underneath would
take tools she didn't have, and time that Jude didn't have. She would

have to take him into the trees—over the lasercams. She took a few minutes to plan her route and practiced scaling the first tree by herself, which was easy enough, but would be a totally different story with an eleven-year-old draped around her. Careful to avoid the tourniquet on his right hand, she heaved his body across her shoulders. She wished she knew how to pray.

She made it to the first branch after only a few failed attempts. Twenty minutes later, drenched in sweat and muscles throbbing, she'd made it up the first tree, above the lasercam. Now for the tricky part: transferring trees.

Samara laid Jude across twin branches to practice going over herself first. She realized she was going to have to do a sort of jump to get across and didn't know how she'd manage with the extra weight. She couldn't worry about that right now, though, and so she jumped.

The branch broke. She fell. She flailed her arms to catch anything. Smaller branches assaulted her face, and heavier ones banged up her legs. She caught one, finally, at the expense of her shoulder. By the sound of it, it was now broken, or at best, dislocated. She looked up and saw Jude's body still lying limply ten or so feet above her. She started to cry, then the cry turned into a scream, and the scream didn't stop until she pulled herself up by her other arm, slowly at first, then with more confidence, onto the branch. She brought herself to rest on it, and finally heard her own scream die off. But what she heard after that wasn't the quiet crickets in the woods. It was another voice.

"I said, Are you okay?"

Her eyes widened and her breath stopped. She looked down to see a woman standing below, directly in the path of the lasercam. But this woman was still intact. She'd disabled them somehow.

"Who are you?" Samara shouted to her.

"A friend." Her voice was rough but not unkind. "You an unreg?"

"Kind of."

"You're close. The safe house is just a little walk thataway. Can you get down?"

"I don't know. My friend and I are both hurt up here. He's farther up than me, and I think he's fainted."

"Stay right there. I'll get some help."

Samara didn't know how long she sat shivering in that tree. When the woman finally came back, Bristol was with her.

CHAPTER TWENTY-FIVE

DENVER WAS SURROUNDED BY NEWS OF THE UNREGISTERED relocation. The voices were everywhere, listing rapidly climbing numbers of unregs being removed from society. The newscasters, who seemed to Denver to be increasingly polished with their red lips and frosted hair, said in throwaway tones that they weren't able to show these unregistered citizens on camera, but being the thorough news team that they were, they had spoken with them, and that the unregs looked forward to creating a society of their own out in New Mexico.

Denver and her mother were both sick when Bristol did not return from work that Tuesday evening. Denver told her to call the moment she heard from Bristol in any way. She waited with impatience, then with mild panic, and finally with rapidly deepening depression. Hours later, Denver's watch shook to signal a phone call.

"Mom?"

"He's gone."

The first hot tears were in her eyes instantly. "He's gone..."

And then they didn't say anything for a long time.

When she was little, Mom used to give them baths in the tub. There'd be bubbles and a yellow duck floating around, but Denver's favorite part was always getting her hair washed. It didn't happen often, so it was rare enough that she looked forward to it all day. Her mother would take a cup—Denver could see it now, blue and plastic with a lip that curved out, just a simple cup ordinarily for drinking juice—and fill it with bathwater. Denver would lean her head back, and her mother would pour water over her, taking care to avoid her face. The water would rush down her hairline and scalp, and sometimes the weight of it would pull her neck farther down toward the water. She'd beg her to do it again, again, three times, four times, five.

He's gone. The words felt like that rushing water over her head, though slower and heavier.

"Mom?"

"Mmhmm?"

"There's something I've been wondering. How did Bristol get here?"

Mom's voice sounded tight. "I gave birth to him."

"I know." Denver sniffed. "I know that. I mean, how? We have to get the focus injections every month. Weren't you getting it?"

"I was. But life finds a way. There are some things in life that you just can't control. Your brother was born because he wanted to live." She let out a low moan, the sound of grief itself.

Denver had so much more to ask her, but there would be time later. They hung up. Alone in the house, she just kept staring at the wall, trying to imagine what her brother was doing or thinking now, the rushing-water feeling coming over her again and again.

She was still there, staring at the wall, when Stephen came home from work. He was returning later and later, and sneaking off in the night, returning before morning, saying he'd been in the bathroom when she was mildly sure he'd just put the light on in there and locked the door. Tonight, she noted, he was especially late, coming in nearly at midnight. Though she didn't have the strength to properly acknowledge him, she did look his way when he removed his shoes and jacket.

"You've been crying."

"My brother..."

He then did something he hadn't done before. He gathered her up in his arms and held her face close to the back of his neck. Without the strength to resist, she allowed it.

"Come to bed and let's talk." Instead of letting her go, he stood with her still in his arms and carried her into their room, where he put her under the blanket and began to dress in his nightclothes. Once in bed himself, he began talking about the relocation—how it was good for the unregs, how it was better for the registered citizens, how there would be more resources to go around now. Of course, this should have made her angry, and did make her angry, but the feeling of sickness was overwhelming, and she just hoped he would stop talking soon so she could sleep and stop feeling things altogether.

When he finally stopped repeating the information he'd heard on the news, she found a light sleep in minutes. And then came a small shake on her shoulder, which she answered without even opening her eyes.

"What, Stephen?"

But it was just another little shake, slightly less patient. She looked at him.

He was wide awake with one finger across his lips. *Shhh.* He got out of bed and turned around so his feet were on the pillow and his head was at the foot of the bed. Brow furrowed and heart beating, Denver turned herself around to meet him. His words were smoke signals, impossible to decipher until they were well in the air.

"Your brother is alive."

"What?"

"Sorry, but I'll explain. Our pillows are fitted with radio microfibers, but not our sheets. They suspect me. I'm pretty sure, anyway. I've run some tests."

"Wait, you're pretty sure our sheets aren't recording us, or you're pretty sure they suspect you?"

Here was his smile. "Both."

"Of what? And how do you know Bristol's alive?"

"They suspect me of being involved with the Red Sea, which I am."

"What's the Red C? What does C stand for?"

"No, *sea*, like the body of water. It's from an ancient myth about a man who took slaves from one country and crossed the sea to liberate them. It's an organization to liberate unregs. I've been involved for years, and I don't know why I haven't been caught, but as long as I'm able to function in society, I'm obligated to help the unregs. I can even work from my watch, but the program is disguised as a game. You know when I told you I'd been outside that night you caught me out of bed? I was at the closest safe house that night. That's where I saw your brother tonight too. The house is along the route to the northern farms."

She was having trouble believing this whole thing. She pinched her own arm, felt the sting, and began to hope. "They didn't get him?"

"No. He's been very lucky, Denver. John Armistead helped him escape."

"Armistead? Armistead..." The movements of her tongue felt familiar at the name, but she couldn't place it.

"You're thinking of Thomas Armistead, one of the New Founding Fathers. He helped create Metrics. John is his disgraced son. He spent years in exile after his father died, and he started talking about a massive reorganization of society. I won't get into it, but eventually he was let back in and punished by being downgraded two tiers. He manages a restaurant, and Bristol just happened to be an employee."

"Oh my God."

"When I saw him, our doctor was just removing his chip. He made it over twenty-five miles with his chip still in, Denver."

"Then they know where he is."

Stephen shook his head and laughed lightly. "You would think so, but he seems to have done this before. He tied a bag of frozen vegetables to his wrist and *ran* with his arm up in the air, all those miles. We don't think Metrics was able to get a signal on him."

Denver laughed too, with her brow all knotted up. His old tricks had saved his life.

Stephen continued. "Listen, though—this part involves you. I'm fairly certain they paired us together because you have an unregistered brother. It's a trap for me. They knew I wouldn't be able to resist. Now that he's missing, they'll be keeping a very close eye on me. And if I'm put in prison, and my tier is taken away—"

"You become an unreg yourself."

"And so does my family, which is you, until you're able to build up your own citizenship score, which would take decades. We'd both be—"

"Relocated."

Now Stephen moved his face closer, his eyes locked on hers. "Killed, honey."

Denver wanted to ask how he knew, but she didn't think she could handle the answer. Anyway, she understood from his face that he was certain.

"Denver, I came back tonight for you. We're married, so if I go down, you do too. But since we're together, our parents are no longer responsible for us. Their score might suffer a little, but they'd otherwise be able to live their lives in peace."

Denver felt as if vines were growing thickly under her skin. Never before had she wished so hard that a conversation hadn't happened, that a day hadn't happened. It was simply too much.

"But we're good citizens! Or at least I am." She was submerged in injustice. "I have worked hard all my life to raise my score, and this is what I get! My marriage is a trap for a traitor!"

"I know it's not fair."

"I need to believe that Metrics has my back." She turned her head to see the pillows, which she felt certain would hear her now. "I'll give you a head start of an hour. Then I'm telling them everything."

"Don't do this."

"Don't waste time, Stephen, and don't worry about me. Metrics will take care of it if I play by their rules."

"You *have* played by their rules, and look where it's gotten you! A brother on the run, a downgraded marriage to catch a rebel. You're playing into their hands, and it's going to get you killed."

Denver said nothing. She turned her body around and lay her head on a pillow. She heard Stephen leaving. The clock turned to 2:15. Fifty-nine minutes to go.

CHAPTER TWENTY-SIX

AT THE SAFE HOUSE, BRISTOL SET A STEAMING CUP OF TEA IN front of Samara but turned away before she made eye contact. Her student was smaller than he'd imagined, but that might have been because he'd been unconscious at their first meeting. Little Jude lay on the sofa, awake but weak, while a short, nut-brown-haired lady, a nurse, gave him sips of water and softly reassured him that he was at Nan's now. That's what this place was called, named for the woman who lived here and operated this little sanctuary. At the moment, the occupants included Nan herself, Lydia—the nut-brown-haired nurse —Bristol, and now, much to Bristol's amazement, Jude and Samara. Lydia seemed downright cheerful that there were so few people here —sometimes there'd be as many as twenty, she'd said—but Nan appeared agitated, constantly looking at her ancient communication device and the sensors on the lasercams to check for little lost lambs in the trees.

The house belonged to Nan, and it seemed to be the complimentary opposite of her personality, like a good marriage. The house itself was on a hill surrounded by pine trees. Other houses were within walking distance, but those other homes seemed like they belonged in a different world than this one. They

were in various stages of repair and disrepair, but one was
meticulously maintained. When Bristol arrived, he'd walked up a
winding gravel path to a clean-swept front porch with neatly
trimmed hedges lining it. The front door to the house was plain
but pleasant. Nan took Bristol around to the back and walked in a
door that looked like the entranceway to an attached greenhouse.
Inside, the only light came from the blazing fire in the fireplace
and from candles strategically placed near mirrors, turning the
rooms bright, soft, and warm. Bristol had seen candles in movies,
but never a real one. Nan told him that Metrics still monitored
their electricity, but there was no way for them to know about the
light from these. They could burn them all night and nobody
would be the wiser. Book-stuffed shelves lined the wall across from
the fireplace. Bristol had never seen a real book before, not the
type with hundreds of pages and hard coverings. He was used to
flimsy bindings, made quick and cheap and easily discarded. He
didn't even know they existed anymore, but here they were, with
yellow pages bound in muted-colored covers. There was a sofa—
the same one Jude was on now—several cots stacked on top of
each other, and several old-fashioned quilts that looked like they
had been stitched together—not with matching patterned patches
of cloth, how wealthy older people liked to make them, but with
all kinds of fabric under the sun. Some patches looked like they'd
come from curtains, some from baby clothes. Bristol even spotted
an elastic band he'd suspected once held underwear on a
man's hips.

Samara was quiet at the table, unmoving. She watched the light
flicker back and forth on the soft brown wood. She still wore her
work clothes, which were stained with mud and torn in places, and
her arm hung in a makeshift sling. Bristol wanted so desperately to
ask her what she was thinking about, if she was in pain, how they
managed to get to Nan's, but a dark shadow of shame intercepted his
words and turned them on him instead. *What do you think she's
thinking about? She wasted her time on you.*

So they both sat at the table across from Lydia and Jude, not

saying anything but listening to the hushed conversation between
Lydia and Nan.

Nan ran her thumb up and down her plastic device's antenna.
"There should be more."

"They're probably scared, or all rounded up by now."

Jude gave a cough, and Lydia brought the water to his lips again
with a little cluck.

"I never saw nothing like this one before."

"There's never been one like this before."

There had been other efforts to clear out unregs, mostly when
new leaders moved into office with their tough-on-crime promises to
keep, but Nan was right—this was the most wide-ranging program
yet. Never had they come into homes and workplaces before.

Bristol cleared his throat. "When will we be moving on?"

"Not for a while, sweet," Lydia answered. "We want to be here in
case there are more coming, and anyway, there'll be lighter border
patrol if we wait."

"How long?"

"Six months? A year?"

Now Samara looked up. "Here for a year? They'll find us."

"Not easily, they won't." Nan shifted her large body. The plastic
sides of her communication device wheezed under the pressure of
her hands. "We got lots of friends in Metrics who keep us up-to-date
on surveillance. And out here, they ain't too concerned about it
anyway."

"Didn't you say you sometimes hosted twenty people at once?
Don't they wonder where those people go? Can't they follow them?"

"We usually know they're coming and disable the chips before
they get to the woods. Metrics lists them as dead on their records,
and no one asks questions. What's a missing unreg here and there?
The way they see it, the fewer of 'em, the better. No, we'll go for the
border when the time's right."

Samara raised her head and licked her lips. "The...border?"

"You didn't think you'd be farming, did you?"

Bristol and Samara looked at each other.

Nan chuckled. "Best-kept secret of the modern age. Of course, you're meant to think the United States of America has taken over the world. You were taught that America had conquered Canada?"

"I was told," Samara said, "that Canada wanted to be a part of us. Wanted to be...great."

"Yep. That's what you were told, all right. And how were you to find out any different? You can't travel. You can't read news that hasn't been filtered through Metrics. You can't talk to anyone who asks questions." She shook her head. "Canada's been the same all along. Different country, just north of us. No system of separating her people either. So you go up there, they'll protect you. You don't have to farm. You can just live. But you gotta stay here awhile first, and be real careful. No electric lights, only food from the garden while you're here. Don't worry, the Red Sea brings us some extra food from time to time. No going outside, no matter what. No loud talking and no singing. Once you're across the border, you can sing to your heart's content."

Bristol stopped for a moment to ponder this. Living with restrictions in order to survive seemed just a different version of the same life, but living without them...living in a place where they could go outside anytime they wanted, day or night, where they could buy whatever food they could afford, where they could live not in a tiered society, but as equals in every outward sense...it was a dream, one that made their hearts beat faster and their minds race, out of habit, to halt hope in its tracks. But it was possible. And perhaps only a few months away.

Samara objected again. "It's different now though, isn't it? They're not just going to write us off as dead. The guards at the prison saw us, and I'm sure we were recorded by lots of street cams coming this way. And that John guy helped Bristol!"

"John Armistead has been punished enough." Lydia's tone was soft but certain. "It might have been different if he'd helped his whole staff, like I'm sure he wanted to, but they won't look into it too much just for helping one boy. His father is still well-respected."

Another wheeze came from Nan's direction. "Besides," she

continued, "they'll have their hands full with the 'relocation,' if you want to call it that. Every policeman in the country won't stop working until they're all dead. It's a good time to lay low. And I don't want to hear any more about it. We'll get to Canada, but we need to spend some time right here first. Just don't go outside, don't go into any other part of the house 'cept the bathroom when you absolutely need it, and don't sing."

Lydia glared at them over her glasses. "We nearly had a riot break out a few years ago when a couple sang 'Row, Row, Row Your Boat' in rounds. They went on for hours."

"What do we do, then?" Samara snapped.

As if to answer, Jude eased up to a seated position and turned his head to look at the wall of books. In the candlelight, it was a treasure chest glistening with emerald and ruby and flecks of gold lettering. They'd never be able to read them all in their time here, not if they started now and didn't ever stop to sleep. A feverish wave washed over Bristol. His body seemed to innately appreciate what this meant —this time, these books—he'd be a different person by the time he left here. Even if he never saw the outside world again, he'd be an adventurer of sorts, a traveler, possibly a connoisseur while he had access to this wall and the power it presented to him.

Nan laughed again in her bass voice. "We can start now." She swung her body to standing and walked over to the shelf. "The best place to begin is the beginning. Bet you don't know how we got into this mess in the first place, do ya?"

"Which mess do you mean?" Jude asked.

"The one we're in now. Some people registered, some not. People only allowed to have one kid. People only being allowed to make small decisions, never any big ones. There was a time before all that. And it wasn't that long ago.

"There was a war in this country in the mid-nineteenth century that people called the Civil War, because it was a war between two sides in the same country."

"What's a—" Samara started, but Nan cut her off with an answer.

"A war was a way to settle arguments, way back a long time ago.

Leaders would force their people to go kill each other, and whichever side killed the most people was thought to have won the argument."

"That's barbaric!" cried Bristol, mirroring Samara's horrified expression.

"Is it? Is it so different from what we're living now? That's the thing about knowing your history, son. The better you know it, the better you can see that we're living in it now. Same problems, same mistakes, different time.

"Anyway, as I was saying, in those days, people had different-colored skin. All people had a different shade, just like today, but the shades were much more..."

"Contrasting," finished Lydia.

"Yeah, contrasting. Some people had dark skin, some people had very dark skin, and other people had light pink skin."

"Light *pink*?" Even after the day he'd just had, Bristol found this hard to believe.

"Kind of a pink-yellow. Look." Nan placed a book down on the table, and there they were, page after page of pictures of people with light pink-yellow skin and multicolored hair. Orange hair, gold hair, brown hair, black hair, all on people with this abnormally light skin. "And that's not all. Some people were dark." She turned a page. Bristol had never seen anyone with skin darker than his, but here was someone with bright teeth and eyes shining up at him.

"So these pictures are from the war?"

"No, no. Much later than that. See, that war was about slavery. One side had the dark people held captive as slaves and made them do all their work for them. They'd tend the fields, and then the lighter skins would make profits off the darker skins and not pay them anything for their troubles."

Bristol could tell Samara had something to say about this but was holding it in. There was so much more to hear.

"The other side wanted all people to live free so no dark skins would ever be slaves again. Guess which side won?"

"By won, do you mean killed more people?" Samara asked.

"Yes. And it was the side with the slaves." Nan's tone was blunt. "Dark skinned people were slaves for over a hundred years after that, but the problem at that point was that they kept comingling so that there were more slaves than owners. And how they were treated got worse and worse. They'd be the ones sent to fight other wars with other countries. They'd have government medical experiments performed on them. There was just no respect for their human lives, never had been, but it was getting more publicized, and most people had relatives—not that they could claim, they mostly kept them private—who had dark skin. And it had to be stopped."

"That's why we're all brown now." Bristol was guessing, but it came out like he knew.

"Yeah, that's why. After Civil War II, the other side won. And they thought there should be no more dark and light, so they changed the laws. Thought there'd be no mistreatment of others if we were all the same color. But did it work? Not at all. Racism was never about skin tones. It was about a group of people thinking they were better and treating another group as lesser, as subhuman. We never needed to be the same color. With the New Race came the Tier system, and before we knew it, we were right back where we started. Ones thinking they were better than the Twos, Twos looking down at the Threes, and so on. It's a nice secure feeling, see, thinking that other people aren't as hardworking or ethical or charitable as you. You start to think you *deserve* it. They could give up their skin colors but they couldn't give up *that* idea. Before, you were allowed to marry anyone you wanted, as long as they had the same skin as you. But after Civil War II, they reversed that—purposely matched people who were different colors so we'd all be the same."

"They were allowed to marry anyone they wanted?" Samara asked. "Didn't they get upset when that was taken away?"

Lydia looked over from the couch where Jude still lay. "No, they didn't. Lots of things had changed by then. Advancements of technology meant that people spent most of their lives connected to people on their devices, but not in life. Most thoughts collected from that time indicated a relief at the pressure being removed from having to find a mate."

Nan nodded. "I think, by that time, most people were on board."

"They were just reverent toward numbers," Lydia continued. "At the time of the revolution, right after Civil War II, people wanted to be able to put numbers on everything. How fast they could run, how many calories they ate, how many people liked them..."

"The numerical generation," Nan added. "It's why we have Metrics today."

Bristol cleared his throat. "Is that when they made the one-child rule?"

"A few years after that, yes." Nan brought down another book, this one with plastic-sleeved pages with loose-printed pages stuffed inside. The one she took out read:

NEW METRIC GOVERNMENT UNVEILS PLAN FOR THE SUPER-GENERATION

Families Now Able to Focus on Raising One Ideal Child

"The important thing to keep in mind was that this *seemed* like a good idea." Nan carefully slid the paper back inside its plastic sheath. "Those were dark times. People were full of hate and competition. They couldn't let it go. It was just part of them, but a part they hated and wanted gone. This was a way to wipe it out."

"It sounds like what's happening now."

Nan's eyes flashed, and she jumped to her feet, jarring Samara's previously undisturbed teacup and sending the hot liquid onto the table, where it shimmered. "That's exactly what's happening now! Don't you see? That's what happens to a people who are ashamed of their history and hide it away. They don't realize that the mistakes, the problems, the attempts at solutions are the same. We're all the same people, underneath our citizenship status, our skin colors, our places in time. And every dangerous idea there's ever been has been sold to the people as a great one."

"They need to know this," Bristol said. "Metrics is made up of people. If those people knew how governments of the past thought they were solving these problems and the consequences that came up..."

"They don't want to hear it. To them, the past is a bore, not a lesson in how to govern." Nan sat back down and wiped the spilled tea with her handkerchief. "Hell, I wish I thought that too. It'd make life a lot easier. But when you know better, you gotta do better. You can't just swim with the current if you know it's headed for a waterfall."

Samara raised her head. "That's how I feel. I'm registered. As terrible as it sounds, there's a part of me that wishes I'd never met either of you. I'd just go on living my life..." she trailed off as Bristol's eyes lowered and Jude bowed his head. Nan nodded and helped her finish her thought.

"If you could go back and not meet them, would you?"

"No," Samara said convincingly. "No, I'd still meet both of them." She looked at Bristol, finally, and he at her. "I'm so sorry. I wouldn't change it."

"That's the thing about truth," Nan said. "You feel the burden of learning it, but you never can unlearn something that's true, and you never want to."

That thought hung in the air for a moment or two and led them into their separate thoughts and fears and dreams until someone began a yawn, which then passed back and forth between them. Nan laid out the thin mattresses and covered them with the hodgepodge quilts and their odd little cushions at the top for them to rest their heads upon. Images of multicolored people drifted behind Bristol's eyes, accompanied by a strange presence of anger, pity, and wonder. He slept without dreaming.

CHAPTER TWENTY-SEVEN

Do it.
Do it.
Do it now.
Now.
No matter how many times Denver repeated these instructions, or how stern she made the voice in her head, her body refused to comply. The anger was easy to come by, because she had betrayed her lifestyle so blatantly by allowing herself to become emotional over what should have been a perfectly rational decision. She never would have considered herself an emotional person. Emotions were detrimental to all aspects of a person's life, and here she was now as proof, physically paralyzed by bits of who-knows-what flying around madly inside her like specks in a decorative snow globe shaken by a wild, unsupervised child.

She lay there on the pillows, bugged or unbugged, until the sun rose behind her curtain. With the dawning of a new day came the realization, blossoming fuller and still fuller in her mind, of the seriousness of what she'd done. Her husband was gone, maybe dead, and maybe not. If he was, she was his killer. If not, then he would be expected at work in an hour, and when he did not come, they would come to question her. And they would ask her why she had not done the thing she'd said she'd do.

As she lay there, curled into a ball with her lips next to the soft fabric of the pillowcase—exactly how she'd positioned herself as she heard Stephen leave the house—she heard something. Running water. She stayed and listened. Yes, it was definitely the sound of the shower. Someone was in the house. After an entire night of paralysis, she slowly put her feet on the floor and made her way toward the bathroom. On the way, she gingerly reached out and curled her fingers around their broom. She held out the handle in front of her as she approached the bathroom, steam from the water floating into the hall from the bottom of the door. She turned the knob, went inside, and whipped open the shower curtain with one hand, thrusting out the broom handle in front of her body with the other.

Stephen didn't seem surprised to see her. After a small scream that seemed to begin to calm while it was still in her throat, she dropped the broom and took two steps back before her knees failed and forced her down onto their fuzzy brown bathroom rug. Stephen, inside the stall, finished rinsing his hair, turned the water off, wrapped a towel around his waist, and stepped out. He crouched beside her on the floor, where, for a moment, neither of them said anything. Finally, Denver could no longer hold the question inside.

"How did you know I wouldn't do it?"

"I didn't."

"I was going to."

"I know."

Then he did something he'd never done before. He reached for her face with both hands and rested his forehead on hers. Aside from Sunday afternoons, she'd never been so near to him before. With his face so close, she could smell cool swirls, like peppermint, and warm ones, like sunshine. She'd always thought that if she was ever so close to a man, she'd feel some sort of exhilaration, an energy that would animate her beyond recognition, but here, feeling his nose grazing hers, and his breath, calm and steady, encouraging hers to match it, she felt only a sense of grounding as she'd never known it. As if she'd been floating and falling her entire life and now was safely on the earth.

He did not move his hands, but put a bit more pressure on the sides of her head, as if he were hugging it, and kissed her forehead. "We don't have much time," he said.

"How long?"

"Well...we don't have any time. See, it's already rush hour, and will be until about ten. If we don't show up for work, they'll check on us. We won't have gotten very far in all the traffic and eyes and cameras on full speed. If we do show up for work..."

"You don't think they'd pick us up there, do you?"

"I do. My boss called this morning to tell me officers were there asking for me."

Denver swallowed. "I'm so sorry. I'm sorry I was afraid."

He squeezed her hand. "We all have moments."

"Why didn't you leave last night?"

Now he looked at her, and now she thought she understood. "Me?"

"You." He laughed softly in his throat. "Do you think I'd risk my life for unregs, most of whom I barely know, and leave my own wife here for dead?"

"Stephen, we barely know each other."

"Yes, but..." he struggled. "Denver, I want to know you. I want to take care of you. I want to be honest with you about where I go and what I do. I want to be your husband."

Here it was. The energy. Suddenly she felt much bigger than her body, and she felt as if she were seeing her husband's face, and only his face, for the first time. Her eyes took in his gentle features and the warmth behind them. She sat on the floor, shocked but absorbed in what he'd said and meant, until a water droplet fell from Stephen's hair onto his cheek and fell like a tear. He wiped it away. "I don't know how to get us out. I'm sorry."

But Denver had already found her feet and was rummaging through the medicine cabinet. She found a pair of scissors and cut two long fibers from the broom.

"What's that?"

"Castor oil." She smiled and held out the two strands from the broom in her fist. "We'll draw straws. One of us is about to be very sick."

An hour later, at the time they were meant to be on their separate trains headed to their separate offices, they were together on the hospital express, whizzing past the traffic carrying men and women in suits to work. She'd never been inside one of these before, but of course she had seen it, the fast-moving red-and-white trains on the highest rail. Inside, the white-tiled walls looked in need of a good scrubbing, and the red, linen-covered seats were pilling and stained. Though she'd never really thought of it before, she realized she'd expected it to be better maintained.

And they really should have brought a bigger bucket, Denver thought as Stephen vomited into the plastic food container she held. When he'd drawn the short straw, she was tempted to take it from him, but upon seeing his excited smile, she could not.

"Sickness bags are located at the front of the car," a cool voice announced over the intercom. Stephen belched.

"It'll be okay. You're doing great." Denver moved her hand in a circular wave over his back before going to get a bag. Neither of them had known how much castor oil to use, so he'd drunk the entire vial. It seemed to be a mistake, though—Denver hadn't expected him to be *this* sick. She remembered the difference between her and Bristol growing up when they were both sick at the same time. Whereas Denver would conserve her energy to get well, Bristol would whine and drag his feet and refuse to get out of bed no matter what degree of illness he was experiencing.

The train came to a halt, the doors opened, and hospital personnel silently and efficiently did their work. Stephen was wheeled to a small room and given fluids through an IV faster than Denver would have liked—as she still needed to work out their escape plan.

"Sorry, hon. Just need to get a blood sample," the nurse said to

Stephen, who at this point was making continuous moaning noises, varying his tone and volume occasionally.

"Ma'am? Your relationship to the patient?" a woman with a tablet asked.

Denver smiled, not taking her eyes off this brave man, this selfless man, her equal. "I'm his wife."

CHAPTER TWENTY-EIGHT

THERE WERE ONLY THREE CHICKENS IN THE YARD NOW, LYDIA had explained. A coyote had gotten the other two last week, poor things. But all was well, as there were exactly the same number of runaways to feed. Samara set one egg aside and cracked the other two in the pan. She watched them sizzle in the heat and wondered why she'd never taken the time to do that before.

Jude was asleep, so he'd have his breakfast later. Lydia and Nan had left early that morning, presumably to their day jobs as a nurse and God-knows-what. Samara scrambled the eggs and pretended not to notice Bristol sneaking glances at her over his book.

"I'm glad you made it here," she said over her shoulder.

He nearly threw down his book. "I am too—I'm glad you and Jude made it."

Samara smiled instinctively as she plated the eggs. "He's a special kid. I wouldn't be here without him."

"He's lucky to have you. You were the one who got him out."

"No, really. I was just moving without a plan, like Chicken Little. I think he would have gotten out by himself, probably in a tidier way if I hadn't helped."

Bristol took the plates and gently placed them on the table. "What happened to his hand isn't your fault."

Samara didn't respond to this. She jabbed a tiny bit of egg and brought it to her mouth. Bristol began to eat too. A few feet away, Jude shifted under his blanket, but his snores remained rhythmic.

"It's my fault," Samara said, "and it isn't. I've been sort of like an accomplice to this whole thing. My whole life, I've just done what I've been told without ever asking why. You're just told 'study for this test' or 'get your injections on time,' but you never ask why. If I hadn't seen with my own two eyes what happened over at the prison, I don't think I'd have believed it. It's just too...outrageous. People can do things in the name of the government that they'd never do as private citizens. And private citizens were who I'd always dealt with."

"Must have been nice."

"What?"

"To just do what you're told. To just trust that someone is looking out for you."

"Well...it was nice, to be honest. I gather you never had that?"

Bristol snorted and moved his elbows outward on the table, seeming to take over the entire side of it. "There were always people telling me what to do, but there was always some underlying subtext. This message, communicated in a thousand different ways, that it didn't matter whether I lived or died. That I was messing things up for people. That maybe it would be better if I wasn't there at all."

"That sounds difficult to deal with."

"Yeah, but I had my mom and my..." Bristol made a sound like a cough and took his elbows off the table again. "My family was the solid part of my life. Like a rock in the middle of the sea. I could always hold on to them."

"Where's your mom?"

"Back in Brookline, close to where you live. She'll be okay. Probably her score will go up now I'm gone."

"And your dad?"

Bristol shook his head and went back to his egg. *So that's why he's unregistered.*

"If I ever get to talk to my parents again, I can ask them to check in on your mom."

"Better ask them to connect with the boy's parents first."

Samara glanced back at Jude, then leaned in and said in a low voice, "I'm not sure how much it would matter. I get the feeling Jude's home wasn't a solid place for him."

"No?"

"When we were coming here, I kept thinking of myself when I was eleven—myself, even as I am today. When I dislocated my shoulder in that tree, I just thought, *I want my mother*. Even now! But Jude didn't say a word about either of his parents. And just the way he talks, the reluctant way he asks for help...I just think he's used to a harder type of love, if he's known love at all."

Bristol cleared his throat. "Maybe that's good."

"Excuse me? He's eleven."

"Sometimes," Bristol began, "love is a burden. It makes us too comfortable. I've been thinking about that, the reason I didn't come with you. See, my family, especially my..." Bristol stared intently into his plate.

Samara wondered, with a clinical fascination, if he was going to cry. She set down her fork. "I know you miss your mom. If you hadn't come, though, she'd be going through a lot worse. She probably thinks you're on your way west, but you know the truth. Maybe you can get back in touch with her one day. Isn't this better?" She stood and took her plate. "I have a family too, you know. A mom and a dad. They have no false comforts. They think I'm dead, but I'm hanging on to the hope that I can see them again someday and explain everything. You're totally wrong about love. It doesn't make you smaller, it makes you bigger. Braver. And real love is seeing who needs it the most, and giving it without hesitation."

Bristol looked up at her, completely dumbfounded. "Me?"

If not now, when?

"Yes, you, brainless." She smiled and shimmied her shoulders slightly, shaking off fear. "You've done more for me than you know. More for everyone than you appreciate."

"I just...I just threw away a napkin."

"Yes, you helped me—and Jude—out of a rough spot. But more than that. You've shown me who you are and who I can be. I've seen the beauty inside your mind, and I fell in love with that beauty."

Bristol appeared to have stopped breathing.

"If you don't want to talk about the wall, we don't have to," Samara said. "But I just wanted to let you know the murals have helped. You've helped. It's the reason I can do this now. They say girls shouldn't think about love. That we have to work twice as hard, be twice as good, to be equal to a man, and that love is a distraction."

Bristol chuckled. "Metrics tries so hard to make men and women equal, but some things are harder to stamp out than others. I know that even when women get married, their friends and family tell to let their husbands make the first moves."

"It's silly. It's outdated. You're the reason I can see that."

Bristol stood up and crossed the kitchen in two steps to reach Samara, but she held her hands out to his chest, stopping him.

"No," she said. "Me first."

She put her hands on his waist, turned him around with his back against the bookshelf, lifted herself onto her toes, and kissed him.

CHAPTER TWENTY-NINE

WHEN NO ONE IMMEDIATELY APPEARED BY THE LAZERCAMS, Denver and Stephen decided to camp for the night. There were supplies, Stephen explained, hidden high in one of the trees. They searched until they saw the sign they were looking for—an orange flag, no bigger than a postage stamp, flapping from a low branch. Denver climbed, discovering new muscle groups in her body as she pulled herself up. She found a pack with a small tent, two blankets, and, thankfully, three large bottles of water. She dropped them to the ground and let herself hang by her arms for a moment before letting go and falling into a pleasant crumple on the ground. She gathered the supplies in her arms and was pleased to find she could carry them all back to Stephen in one trip, if she made an effort. He was sitting on the ground a few feet away with his head in his hands. She picked up one of the bottles and extended it toward him.

"Drink this now."

He followed orders without hesitation. When he had emptied the bottle, Denver handed him the second one.

"I shouldn't," he said. "What if there are more people coming?"

"You're dehydrated. You need it now. Besides, I saw another supply tree on my way back."

"Okay. Let me just catch my breath. I'm afraid I might puke it back up."

"Just relax," said Denver. "I'll set up camp."

Stephen lifted his head. "Do you know how?"

Denver paused, considered lying, then decided she'd had enough of that. "No. But I'm not going to let that stop me. Just focus on not puking, please."

Denver took the tent and searched until she found a collection of brambles growing thickly. She went inside, rearranging the twisted vines until she'd fashioned a small clearing. She set up the tent with more patience than she expected of herself and then covered the top in vines. She went back for the blankets and laid them along the tent's green vinyl floor. When she returned for Stephen, he was leaning against a tree trunk with the second bottle in his hand, now only half-full.

"Feeling better?" Denver asked.

"A little. Don't go over there," he said, pointing in the distance and lowering his head. "I..."

"Don't worry, I know. It's okay."

"I didn't think it would hit me like that."

"I probably should have been the one to take it. I'm more used to it."

Stephen's eyes widened. "You've done this before? Made yourself sick on purpose?"

Denver nodded. "It's an old trick to lose weight fast. It flushes everything out, gives you diarrhea, dehydrates you like crazy. They try to tell us that all that matters is hard work, but girls see pretty quickly that there are other things that can give you a leg up."

"That's insane. And dangerous."

"I know," she said quietly. "I'm beginning to see that." The whole world was insane and dangerous."

Stephen eyed her and took another drink. "It'll be good to get to Nan's. They must have just missed the six o'clock sweep, but someone will be here tomorrow morning to look for us."

"Can you walk? The tent's over there." Denver ducked under Stephen's shoulder to steady him. She led him toward the thicket.

"Nice disguise!" Stephen said when he saw it.

Denver smiled and felt a flush of pride. "So is this what you've been doing? Packing up camping supplies and hiding them in the woods?"

"Sometimes. Mostly I just work on wiping evidence from Metric's surveillance systems."

"Like the systems I monitor at the DA?"

"Mon*itered*. And yes, sort of. I erase energy usage from the safe houses sometimes. I rewired my watch to project my own game history when I work so if anyone sees me—"

"—It'll seem like you're being a good citizen, working on a high score in his free time." Denver laughed. "I wondered why it was taking you so long to get to level five on *Bedazzled Battles*!"

They laughed together and ducked into the tent. They looked at each other for a fraction of a second, then made identical motions toward their wrists. Denver jumped involuntarily when she felt bare skin under her fingers.

"That's going to take some getting used to," she said, gliding her fingertips over her wrist.

"I was thinking the same thing. Funny how we're both so used to being around the unregistered. They don't have watches and we just think that's normal. Just expect them to function at the same level we do."

"They're probably better for it. My brother has never even seen an art program—you know the ones where you can draw pictures and then get it all to automatically correct itself? The lines get straighter and the shadows get more realistic and that kind of thing? But he can draw some amazing things just with his hands."

"I know," Stephen said. "I've been keeping the cameras off that kid for years. He's very good. Very influential."

"Influential?"

"I don't think he knows it, but the Red Sea has gotten stronger since he's been painting. We've gotten lots more members because of his work."

"Like, unregistered people coming to you for help?"

"No, I mean registered people helping them. They see your brother's paintings and it's like some sort of a switch goes off. Like they're not alone. Someone else is seeing just how absurd everything is and they have to do something about it."

"Is that what happened to you? Why are you involved?"

"No, I've been at this for a long time. My mom was involved. One time she missed a meeting and they arrested everyone. She was home, sick with a cold. Two of the members, a husband and wife, were both taken and their five-year-old son was arrested too."

Denver's brow furrowed. "And charged with what?"

"Probably preventative detainment. They don't need a good reason. Any reason at all will do." Stephen curled onto his side. "So that's when my mom told me what she'd been up to. She thought I needed to know, for my own safety. Once I had the chance to think about it, I decided I wasn't just okay with it, I wanted in." He smiled weakly. "I just heard about your brother a few years ago, when all our new recruits were asking who was doing the murals on their kid's school building or their bus stop."

"If you knew who he was..." Denver started to ask, "Did you know who I was too?"

His smile became broader. "I did."

Denver moved her gaze around the tent, thinking rapidly. "Did you fix our marriage? Are we married so you could be close to my brother? Were you planning this the whole time?"

"No! No to all that. I just thought...well, I thought you were beautiful, and then I saw you applied for marriage and thought we might be good together so..."

"So you fixed it."

He sat up. "No, but not for lack of trying. The New Race is way too important to Metrics to let a rookie hacker like me break into the pairing assignment system. In the end, all I could do was add myself to the list of your potential pairs. The list was over three hundred names long. It was an enormous long shot."

Denver snorted. "And what? It just worked out?"

He took her hands. "After I put my name on your list, I promise I had nothing to do with it. Sometimes, things just work out."

Denver looked down at his hands and drew a circle around his wrist. "What did you think when you got the assignment letter?"

He squeezed her hands tight. "Before today, it was the happiest day of my life."

CHAPTER THIRTY

SOMETHING INSIDE JUDE HAD BEEN ROUSED FROM ITS SLEEP. THE first night in Nan's expansive library, this thing—this rage, this darkness—had started to lift its quiet head. After only a few days on the sofa, fed by this pirate's horde of knowledge, it had begun to pace, to snarl, to roar.

Always shy and sheepish in the face of criticism in the past, the old Jude may have been content to sit on Nan's sofa, feeling sorry for himself when he happened to catch a glimpse of where his hand used to be. Now he saw it and his blood boiled. He deserved it, he told himself. He should have warned Kopecky about his suspicions of the warden, and he didn't. He must have been too afraid, or too trusting. If he'd just thought a little quicker, he might have been able to ask Miss Shepherd to smuggle them both out. Surely she'd have been able to. They'd stuffed Kopecky into a bag like he didn't matter at all, like he was a piece of trash to be removed. They'd pay for this, Jude thought for the hundredth time from his sofa in front of the hearth, if it was the last thing he did. In the meantime, he read hungrily, an involuntary growl turning into a bark when the book whipped shut from his awkward one-handed grip. He thought Nan might reprimand him for being loud, but she only sat next to him, picked up his book, and read to him in a slow, even meter. She stayed as long as she could before she left for the afternoon to check the lasercams once again.

"We've got a long way to go," Miss Shepherd reminded him in her teacher voice as Nan left. She sat beside Jude's feet on the sofa. "Just take it slow."

"Kopecky thought he had time too," he said in a sharp voice he didn't recognize. "We may not have as much time as we think, Miss Shepherd."

"You can call me Samara now, if you like." She picked up the book Nan had been reading from. "Chapter six?"

Jude nodded and fell back into his pillows, which had gone flat under his back.

"Hold on," said Lydia before Samara could start. She turned to Bristol. "Are you the Hope?"

Bristol, Samara, and Jude all turned their heads, unsure of the question's target. Jude asked, "The what?"

"The Hope." Her eyes were on Bristol. "I saw you working on that." She nodded toward the stack of papers turned down on the table where Samara was sitting. Bristol lunged, but Samara got there first. When she unfolded the paper, Jude looked over her shoulder: it was a pencil drawing of Samara reading aloud. At least he thought it was Samara: there was outline of her body, vague but unmistakable, hunched, as she must have been when Bristol began sketching, and the light strokes of the pencil somehow perfectly reflected how the candles were flickered against the darkness. The movement of the candlelight—it was the same movement Jude had seen in the graffiti on the wall the night he was arrested: the blood dripping from the woman's hand.

"Is that what they're calling him now?" asked Samara, still surveying the drawing, still letting her eyes dance on the page along to the music that was that flickering light. "The Hope?"

"Only in certain circles," answered Lydia. "So, is it you? Are you the one gracing our fair city's walls with your graffiti?"

Bristol swallowed. "No."

"No?"

"Well, I mean, I paint. But I'm not...what you said. I can't be the only one doing this."

"No, I think you are," said Lydia. "Nan and I keep up with these things. They usually catch graffiti artists quick. I mean, they always say they catch someone, but the poor souls who actually go to jail over them are more than likely innocent bystanders. Wrong place, wrong time. You can tell when they've caught the real artist when the paintings stop. And yours haven't." She paused and eyed Bristol. "So, are you? This sure looks like the same work."

Jude's insides flashed cold. He slowly turned to Bristol, every cell in his body screaming injustice. "You."

"I never meant for anyone to get hurt."

"Too late for that!" Jude yelled, holding up the stump of his wrist. "And some of us are dead! My friend died this week for something he didn't do—he got caught up with people like you, people who don't care who lives and who dies, who just want to go on doing what they like! *Painting pictures!*"

"Bristol's not the one who sent you to prison, Jude." Samara's voice was calm, but her posture was fierce. "You were sent there because they didn't understand you and didn't want to. They didn't know how to measure your value, and so they thought you didn't have any. You and Bristol have a lot more in common than you think."

Jude stewed, his only fist clenched on his lap. "I wouldn't do something, even if I loved it, knowing it could get someone hurt. There's no reason to do something so dumb."

"You'd be surprised what art can do, young man." Lydia smiled and rocked harder in her chair. "Art can tell us the truth, draw back the curtain, expose the lives we've been living—and the lives we wish we lived. No, they don't like art, not at Metrics. And they don't want us to like it, either. They want us to like games and money and promotions and new things for our houses. They want us to like the art they print and sell and put in frames for our walls. Pictures of flowers and celebrities. They know that if enough people like art—

real art, art that educates them, comforts them, inspires them—then it's all over."

Jude licked his lips. "So why not end it?"

"Sorry?" Bristol asked.

"If your art inspires people, why not paint something that will inspire them to overthrow Metrics? Paint history, what we learned here! Paint the pink people killing the brown people. Paint a map that shows Canada. Tell them about this whole mess, and we can start to build a movement!"

Bristol rested his elbows on his knees and ran a thumb over his fingertips. "That's not why I do it, Jude."

"Why wouldn't you do that? What can be more important?"

"I just do it...so I know I exist."

Everyone considered this in a beat. Jude got the feeling he wasn't the only one who didn't understand. "What?"

Bristol fidgeted. "Creating these things...even if I hate them afterward...it lets me know that I'm really here. The act of creating is what does it, not the end result. I usually hate the end result."

"But you still put them on buildings for everyone to see," said Jude. "Your personal thoughts, blown up on buildings—you must not hate them that much."

"Hate isn't the right word. I know that they're imperfect, but not letting anyone see them seems unfair to them and to the time I spent letting myself know I'm really here."

"I don't think proving your own existence is a good enough reason to do it. Can't you just paint one picture?" Jude heard the whine of a child in his own voice. "For the greater good?"

"Listen to what you're asking. The whole of Metrics was conceived for 'the greater good.' I don't want to build a movement. I just want to be in a place where I can be myself. Up until this point, that place has been in my notebook or on a brick wall."

Samara looked up at him. "If you think that makes you a hero, it doesn't."

Bristol wilted visibly.

"I knew it was you. Your murals made me think about things I wanted to ignore. It made me brave. But now—knowing you only did it to make yourself feel important—well, I shouldn't be surprised."

"Samara—"

"No, listen. I shouldn't be surprised because I knew it was you and I thought you were trying to protect me by not telling me. Jude's got a point. I was willing to defend you when I thought you were painting things so others would think about them, but I can't condone what you've done knowing it was just to benefit yourself. I took a chance for you. You nearly got us killed. Both of us." She nodded to Jude.

Bristol closed his eyes and didn't speak.

Nan's radio crackled and all heads turned to listen. It was very touchy, this radio, and somehow it helped to look at it. It crackled again, and they could hear Nan's unintelligible voice behind the static. It sounded urgent but not afraid. A word like *mother*, or *other*...

Lydia stiffened. "Cover."

"What does it mean?" asked Samara.

"It means they're coming here. It means hide."

Lydia flew to the bookshelf and felt for something between the shelves. When she found it, she curled her fingers and pulled. Part of the bookshelf opened like a door, narrowly and quietly, so as not to disturb the books it had been tasked with holding up. Behind the door that looked like a bookshelf was a small opening like a closet, with just enough room for the three runaways. Bristol put his hands on Samara and guided her into the space, but she broke away and reached for Jude. Seeing her reach for him, Jude had the thought that Samara was getting bigger by the hour, and he was getting smaller. He thought of his mother, how big she'd always seemed, larger than life, and missed her despite his certainty that she wouldn't have reached for him in the way Samara did. Lydia drew a breath and closed the bookshelf, leaving the three engulfed in darkness.

Lydia's boots paced back and forth, and Jude noted where she was in the room by the pendulum pattern of resonance of the wooden floor and the shush of the worn woven rug. After what seemed a long time, the pacing stopped. Then it started again. Her feet were just about to begin another round of shushing when there was a piercing rap on the door. Not the front door, but the door to the back room.

"Hello?" Lydia answered.

And that was all. No explanation, no scream. Just a sweet and inquiring "Hello?" and Lydia's voice was gone, accompanied only by the sick notion they'd never hear it again. What they did hear, however, were the sounds of the room being destroyed. They heard the mirrors being broken, the furniture being thrown down, and finally, the books on the shelves being violently hurled across the room. With every pitch, Jude's body flinched until he felt Samara's reassuring hand on his right shoulder and Bristol's on his left. He turned around to bury himself in their embrace and realized they'd been holding hands. They broke and held on to him and each other tightly as war waged just inches away.

And then, without words, there was a murderously thick sound next to them, on the far end of the naked bookshelf.

"Ax," Bristol whispered.

Desperately, Jude looked around in search for a miracle. "What's that?" he whispered back, pointing to the wall behind them.

Samara reached up and touched the mysterious rectangle. "I don't know, but we might be able to go through it."

Bristol pried open the grate, and they wordlessly lifted Jude into the small space. It was a sort of metal tunnel, which, with any luck, would lead them away from the rampage. He had no time to wish he'd read more about historical architecture to understand what a thing like this was doing in a house or to wonder whether Samara and Bristol would fit in this small space after him. He only knew he had to do his best to sprint, on his knees and his one hand, toward the unknown. His speed surprised him, and soon he came upon another opening into what looked like a bedroom. He turned around to see Samara and Bristol behind him.

"Go," whispered Samara.

He pushed open the grate and landed on what had to be Nan's

gigantic bed. He knew it was hers just as surely as he knew it had been purposely placed there for just such an escape.

"Window," he said when the others were down. He could smell something burning in the back of the house as smoke wafted through the opening they'd just come from.

They climbed out the window and ran into the forest, which seemed to open its arms in a dark welcome.

CHAPTER THIRTY-ONE

SAMARA WAS PANICKING. "WHY DIDN'T THEY SEE US?" SHE WAS still panting from their run into the woods. "Why didn't they follow us?"

"Because they weren't people," answered Jude simply, and then he laughed. "I'm sorry—does it seem funny to you that we've survived this long? They've had so many chances!" He laughed again.

Bristol and Samara exchanged looks.

"No, no," said Jude. "I know about this one. My mom works in the Department for Defensive Robotics. They build these robots for situations that might be dangerous for people to be in and they only give them one or two specific purposes, a very clear mission—to cut down on unintended consequences. They knew Lydia was there, but I don't think they knew we were, They must have had instructions to remove Lydia and to destroy the safe house."

"Remove?" asked Samara.

They were silent for a moment, and then Bristol took a step toward Samara. "I think we should probably..."

Jude tried to finish for him. "Move forward, assuming Lydia and Nan are..."

"They must have known about the network. The other safe houses might be in danger," Samara finished.

"We have to get to Canada," Bristol said.

Jude laughed again, more cynically this time. "Without watches or even a radio? Even a paper map could be helpful. Why didn't we think to look for one in a book while we had them?"

Samara thought of the books a moment, and of the candles and the soft quilts at the place that no longer existed. She shook off the memory. "Well, we didn't. And we have to get there. So what now?"

Jude sniffed. "The Red Sea. There have to be other safe houses somewhere."

No one said what they all knew to be true. They had no way of finding them, if they had existed in the first place and survived the relocation efforts. Instead, the three of them walked a long time in the aging forest, moving slowly to avoid snapping the twigs on the ground. The trees seemed to offer a primal protection from human surveillance, covering them with dark shade and occasionally spilling streams of sunlight on their feet. Samara watched her feet move along the forest floor and allowed herself to be hypnotized by the shades of green and brown.

Bristol broke the spell as he stopped and pointed to some large rocks in the distance. When they approached them, they found a flowing stream and a small cave.

"We can hide here until someone comes to find us."

Jude's voice was quick and high-pitched. "How would someone find us? Nan deactivated our chips."

"I don't mean Metrics. I mean others who are looking for the Red Sea."

"And how would they find us?" asked Samara.

"I'm going to draw some pictures. Make some signs."

Samara shook her head. "Is that...wise?"

"How else are we going to find the safe houses?"

Bristol went to work. Samara could hear the pride in his voice as he instructed Jude on how to make a fire.

"Who taught you this?" Jude asked.

"Denver," he replied. "She was in the Girl Survivor League when we were kids."

When Samara asked who Denver was, however, Bristol simply cleared his throat, bowed his head, and walked away to gather more sticks. The flames were small, but Bristol kept them alive. He picked out the charred pieces and mixed them with water to create a thick black paste. Then he put out the fire, dipped his finger in the paste, and stood in front of the wide rock at the mouth of the cave.

Samara watched as he shifted his weight from side to side. He made careful lines first, and then filled in the spaces with lightness in his hand. He cocked his head to the side as if trying to see something invisible, then moved his arm up and down on the rock. He worked until dark, until the star-made shadows completely covered his work. He stood back and crossed his arms.

"What is it?" Samara asked.

"It's...a rock." said Jude.

It certainly was. Far from actually drawing anything with the ashes, Bristol had only accentuated the natural shadows and lines on the stone, making it appear more like a stage prop than something found in nature.

"See these lines here? And here?" Bristol gestured to the top lefthand corner. "These aren't natural shadows. Especially tomorrow afternoon, it'll look all wrong. Hopefully it'll be enough to catch a human's eye..."

"But it won't be obvious enough to get the attention of any drones that might fly overhead." Jude's smile was wide and his eyes, focused on Bristol, glittered. "Brilliant!"

Bristol looked at Samara, perhaps expecting her to echo the compliment. She only looked down. "Let's just see if it works."

The next day, they caught fish for breakfast. Though none of them had ever eaten meat before—it was punishable under Metrics—they were hungry enough to try the techniques they'd only seen in old movies. Cowboys would grab swimming fishes with their bare hands, roast them over an open fire, and eat them as if it were the easiest thing in the world. In reality, these tasks took the three of them the better part of two hours, and when they had eaten, their stomachs growled for more.

"Why don't they teach us survival skills in school?" Jude asked Samara.

"Maybe they hope we'll never need them," Samara answered.

"Or make it harder for us if we do," Bristol said with a glum look at his rock.

Samara's eyes were suddenly wide. "Shh!"

They were suddenly as silent and still as the forest. Then they heard the sound of humans. Leaves rustling, faint conversation. Bristol stamped on the feeble fire, and they hid in the cave.

"Where are they coming from?" asked Samara.

"Just around those trees. We'll see them in a second," Bristol answered.

Samara saw, among the twisting branches growing skyward, a couple walking along the stream. The young woman walked in front of the man, and they were chatting in light, easy tones.

"Do you think they're—"

Before Samara could finish her sentence, Bristol ran for the girl and they crashed into each other with a tight embrace.

"I knew we'd find you," she said hoarsely.

The young man stepped forward. "We saw the smoke and then the rock," He regarded Bristol, then turned to Samara. "I'm Stephen. This is my wife, Denver."

Samara looked again at Denver and knew the shape of her body and face and hair. *Something blue.*

"My sister," Bristol choked as he roughly wiped a tear.

"I'm Samara, and this is Jude."

"I know. I've heard so much about you," answered Denver, like a guest at a dinner party.

Samara glanced at Bristol, whose cheeks were just beginning to turn a shade of red when Samara had another thought.

"How did you get away?

"Oh, that turned out to be much easier than we expected," said Denver.

Stephen rolled his eyes. "Maybe for *you*."

"Well, we did have to make Stephen sick enough for the hospital so we'd both have a place to be that wasn't work or home. We checked in, they gave Stephen fluids, and then when we left, we just put our watches on the trains going downtown and Stephen took us here." Denver grew breathless and turned her eyes up to Stephen's smiling face. "If they check in on us, they'll still find us riding around on the train—around and around. We hid out for a couple of days in another safe house closer to town. I didn't realize how sick he'd really be."

"I'll live. And of course, they'll be on to us by now." Stephen frowned. "I take it Nan's place is no longer in operation?"

Jude swayed beside Samara. She pulled him into an awkward side-hug.

"That's right," answered Bristol, and he explained what had happened. Stephen and Denver listened, their light and airy faces growing longer, their eyes growing more centered, their lips tighter.

"So what should we do?" asked Jude when Bristol had finished, still clearly a bit suspicious of these new additions.

Stephen considered a moment. "There is an emergency plan. I don't know whether it's too early for it to have been implemented or not, though—but for our sake, the earlier, the better.

"If what you've said is true and the network is being systemically destroyed, the emergency volunteers are called to drive on the roads with some sort of red insignia on the transport."

"Where on the transport?" asked Samara.

"And what kind of transport?" asked Bristol.

"It's purposefully vague," Stephen explained. "We just have to keep sharp, and look, and trust. It could be a car, or a motorbike, or a bus. It could have a driver, but it doesn't have to. It could be a strip of tape on the hood, or a ribbon on the mirror, or the whole thing could be painted red."

A collective gulp.

"We don't have a chance," Bristol said.

"We do," said Samara. "Stephen's right. We've made it this far. We'll know whether or not it's right when we see it."

"We have to try," added Jude.

Bristol snickered. "Why?"

"Because we're here. We exist, we matter, we deserve to live." With this, Samara reached inside her pocket for a folded piece of paper and put it inside Bristol's hand. He recognized his sketch of her sitting hunched there in the candlelight, reading to her little friend.

"We need to get to a road," Denver said.

They walked through the forest for a few hours, each moving back and forth between giving themselves internal speeches on the importance of going on and taking time to be thankful for the breath in their lungs and the blood in their bodies and the thoughts in their minds while they all were still present. Eventually they came to a road, a crumbling, ancient-looking one with no paint or lights.

"What do we do now?" asked Jude.

Stephen never took his eyes off the road. "Wait."

They waited. After several hours, they heard the sound of wind rushing around something moving fast. Two headlights, colored red, appeared in the distance. Stephen drew a breath and stepped out onto the road. The car slowed to a stop. There was no driver, but the doors were unlocked. Stephen opened a door and looked expectantly at the little group.

Samara stepped inside first, into the back. Bristol laid his hands heavily on Jude's shoulders, guiding the boy inside to sit between them in the back of the cab. Denver and Stephen slid into the front seat. Stephen closed the sliding door, and the car started again down the crumbling road, driving them forward—they hoped—to freedom.

Long after the sun had set, Bristol's eyes burned with exhaustion while they took in the dark shapes of trees and fields whipping by. If any of them felt confident about where they were headed, nobody said so. Stephen was straight-backed and focused on the road, though his arm rested on the seat and Denver rested her head on it, asleep. Jude was also asleep, with his face pointed up, his head straight back, and his mouth hanging open. Bristol and Samara stared out their respective windows. Bristol felt a staleness had set in. The time for hope and gratitude had passed, as had the time for anxiety. This was just a time for waiting.

They waited hours until the car began to slow. Within seconds, Bristol noticed the change, though he suspected he was the last to do so. Stephen and Samara had already leaned forward and were looking from side to side.

"What's happening?" whispered Samara.

"It's running out of battery," Stephen said.

"What are we going to do?" asked Bristol.

Stephen looked back at him. "I don't know."

The car continued down the country road for just a few minutes more before puttering to a stop. The red headlights flickered and died. None of them had experienced the total blackness of the country night before. It woke Denver and Jude.

"Car died," explained Stephen, and he made a movement to leave.

"You can't see anything out there," Denver said.

"I'm going to go anyway. In fact, let's all go. Our eyes can adjust to the light of the moon and stars eventually. Won't be enough light to look at the car, but at least we can get off the road."

Shuffling reluctantly, the five of them were soon out in the cool night air. Next to him, Samara gave a brief shiver and crossed her arms. Bristol wished he had a coat to offer. Stephen was saying something about a checkpoint being close, but Bristol no longer cared. They would get there or they wouldn't. They would survive or they would die. At this point, he lived only in the now, and there was nothing he wanted more than to comfort Samara. He made a motion to put his arm around her waist.

Without warning, the car's headlights blazed a clear white color and it sped off far into the distance.

They froze. Samara spoke first. "It's a trap!"

"It's not," Denver said.

Before Samara could challenge her, she heard what Denver heard —music. With their eyes still blinded by oppressive darkness, they heard a group in the distance, singing:

When Israel was in Egypt's land:
Let my people go,
Oppress'd so hard they could not stand,
Let my people go.
Go down, Moses,
Way down in Egypt's land,
Tell old Pharaoh,
Let my people go.

THE END

Thank you for reading! Find book 2 of the Unregistered series coming soon. For more from M. Lynch, check out her website and join the mailing list.

Facebook: www.facebook.com/mlriggs

Twitter: www.twitter.com/mlynchbooks

Instagram: www.instagram.com/m.lynch.books/

Website: www.mlynch.net

Please sign up for the City Owl Press newsletter for chances to win special subscriber-only contests and giveaways as well as receiving information on upcoming releases and special excerpts.

All reviews are **welcome** and **appreciated**. Please consider leaving one on your favorite social media and book buying sites.

For books in the world of romance and speculative fiction that embody Innovation, Creativity, and Affordability, check out City Owl Press at www.cityowlpress.com.

ACKNOWLEDGMENTS

Any creation, I've learned, has not one but many creators, and this book is no exception. Without my wide network of support, this book would be doomed to my desktop. Then my computer would crash (technology isn't my strong suit), and then there'd be no book at all.

First I should thank Ryan, who always believes in me and teaches me things I insist I can't do, like backing up my work on the external hard drive. Thanks for not believing me when I tell you how much smarter you are than me, even though you're smart enough to realize it's probably true.

To my two babies, Finnegan Dean and Clark Francis. You've both introduced the concept of working under pressure in my life, and I genuinely enjoyed writing this book (and the sequel) at the furious pace I did, praying you wouldn't wake from your nap until I finished another paragraph.

To my family: Mom, Dad, Nanny, Brian, Kevin, Jamie, Dianne, Rich, Lindsay, Tim, Elissa, and especially Michael, who (bless him) read and thoughtfully reviewed the first draft of Unregistered. Thank you all for listening to me ramble about this project and for loving me anyway.

To my editors, Jennifer Chesak, Michael Phillips Mann, Amanda Roberts, and Jo Vanderhooft, and the entire team at City Owl Press. Thank you all for your eagle eyes and poignant suggestions, and for being encouraging advocates along the journey to publication. I'm fortunate to have a band of editors who share my love of these characters and ask deliberate questions to strengthen them. You've all made me both a better writer and a better reader.

And to the readers. Those of us that have discovered the love of reading have discovered one of life's purest joys. I'm glad to share it with you.

ABOUT THE AUTHOR

M. LYNCH lives in Nashville, Tennessee with her husband and her sons, Finnegan and Clark. Her debut dystopian novel, Unregistered, depicts the underside of a utopian society when some members live on the fringe and don't fit in. In addition to writing, she loves reading, running, yoga, music, and human rights.

Facebook: www.facebook.com/mlriggs

Twitter: www.twitter.com/mlynchbooks

Instagram: www.instagram.com/m.lynch.books/

Website: www.mlynch.net

ABOUT THE PUBLISHER

City Owl Press is a cutting edge indie publishing company, bringing the world of romance and speculative fiction to discerning readers.

www.cityowlpress.com

CPSIA information can be obtained
at www.ICGtesting.com
Printed in the USA
BVOW08s0545080917
494271BV00001B/76/P